AWAKENING

THE EDITED GENOME BOOK 1

MARCOS ANTONIO HERNANDEZ

ISBN-13: 978-1-7320035-8-3 (Paperback edition)

ISBN-13: 978-1-7320035-7-6 (Ebook edition)

For G. Hudson Drakes, who encouraged me to write this story.

For Melissa... you know what you did.

CHAPTER ONE

THERE's something sinister in the laws of evolution.

Some people, through no fault of their own, find themselves cast below others from the first breath they take. The ones whose parents and ancestors have struggled to adapt are required to scratch and claw for every bit of slack they take from the tether of their existence.

Once technology was created to allow humans to make their offspring happier, healthier, and smarter, a clear split was created between those who could afford the procedure and those who had to wait for nature to catch up.

Edited humans, not wanting their lineage's DNA to revert to the natural state, sequestered themselves in compounds in order to safeguard the wealth they had acquired through generations of increased productivity. The unedited were forced to live in cities and scrape out whatever existence they could while hoping to afford edits to their own children as a perverse retirement plan.

Shada Gray knew she was different because she didn't want children. All she wanted was to play in the league and make enough money to help her sister, Sikya, afford to edit a future child. It wasn't uncommon for professional athletes to set their children up by paying for embryos to be edited before birth, and since Sikya had wanted to be a mother for as long as either of them could remember, it only made sense for Shada to help.

Those dreams were dashed by a five-minute conversation with Shada's coach before practice one summer morning.

"We might have a problem," Coach Patrick said after asking her to sit down across from him at the desk. He was taller than Shada by a head when standing but the same height when they both sat down. Trophies from past victories sat on shelves next to team photos from years past.

"You know how your contract was dependent on your blood coming back clean?"

Shada nodded.

"Well, it appears your levels of hemoglobin are outside the acceptable range."

Shada stared at him, her expression blank.

"Hemoglobin allows for more oxygen to be transported to your muscles," Coach said.

"I know what hemoglobin does," Shada snapped back.

Coach squeezed his lips together and nodded. "I have to ask you this: Have you been blood doping?"

"No! I could never afford it, and even if I could I wouldn't do it."

"So this is natural. This is what we feared. It's why you were dominant in school—"

"Not dominant enough for them to give me a scholarship."

"But dominant enough to get a tryout and make a pro team," Coach said, expressing patience in his now-relaxed face. "It'd be simpler if you were doping. You would be suspended for a few months and could then join the team."

Shada waited for her coach to continue. They'd worked

together for a few short weeks but had already managed to settle into a comfortable coach-athlete relationship.

"But since this is natural, and it falls outside the acceptable range, you won't be able to play professionally. In this country, at least."

Shada got the sense she was falling backwards, like she leaned too far back in her chair and couldn't catch herself. Her mind raced, trying to find a way around this roadblock.

"What if I got it edited into the acceptable range?"

"There can't be any edits whatsoever to hemoglobin levels. League rules."

"So there's nothing I can do?"

"I'm afraid not."

Shada wanted to scream, wanted to launch into a tirade about how unfair the situation was, wanted to demand a solution from her coach even though she could tell from his tone of resignation no solution existed. Instead, she tucked her chin, lowered her head, and took ten deep breaths through her nose and felt the air deep in her belly, a trick she'd learned as a child from her father before he passed away. It had helped calm her down when he died, and it helped calm her down after her dreams were shattered in the coach's office.

Silence enveloped the room before Shada lifted her face. Coach seemed surprised her cheeks were dry; no tears had been shed.

"Thank you for the opportunity," Shada said. She stood up and shook hands with her coach.

"Look into playing overseas. They aren't as strict about genetic differences," Coach said.

"Good to know," Shada said. She was thankful she hadn't put her bag in the locker room before their chat, because now she could walk out without seeing any other athletes and didn't have to explain why she wouldn't be seen at practice anymore.

The sun shone through a cloudless sky and hit Shada's face outside the training facility. She squinted through the ripples of heat emanating from the cars lining the road, most of which hadn't moved in the weeks she'd practiced with the team. Beads of sweat gathered on her forehead as she walked to the train station alongside commuters on their way to work. She pulled out the bag of red gummy bears she saved for after practice every day and ate one at a time. Sikya couldn't stand how much candy she ate, so she took it upon herself to provide Shada with an apple every morning, an apple Shada made a habit to give away to the homeless man on her way to practice.

The train was packed, but Shada found an empty seat next to the window and stared at the buildings that passed by with increased frequency as the train gathered speed. An ad for financed genetic edits by WestCorp, by far the largest DNA editing operation and owner of the island compound just outside the city, was plastered on the side of one of these buildings. She had considered investigating post-birth edits, but they were rumored to cost as much as Shada's entire education. No reason to double her debt when it wouldn't help her get into the league.

The seat next to her opened up for a moment at the next stop before a broken old lady boarded the train and approached. The two tennis balls on the ends of the legs of her walker had been attached for so long that the bright green fuzz was worn away, leaving dull beige rubber to precede each of her uncertain steps.

"Is anyone sitting here?" Tennis Balls asked, pointing to the seat on Shada's left.

Most old white ladies didn't ask to sit next to women with brown skin, they just sat down. Shada shook her head, and the woman managed to sit down right before the train began to move again.

A hand spotted with age gripped the handle of the walker as they picked up speed. "Lovely day today, isn't it?" Her smile was too white and matched her colorless hair.

Shada gave the woman a thin-lipped smile, nodded, and wondered how many of those teeth were fake before she turned to look at the graffiti now passing outside her window. Less than an hour ago she had been making the reverse trip on her way to practice. Her future had almost been secure.

"Where are you heading?" the woman asked.

"Home."

The old lady nudged Shada's backpack, which was on the ground next to the walker, with her foot. "Coming back from school?"

Shada wanted to say something about how, if she was, the class must have started at dawn. Instead, she turned and informed the woman she'd graduated last spring.

"Congratulations!"

"With a mountain of debt," Shada said. Then, under her breath, "And no way to pay it off."

"But nobody can ever take away your education," the old lady said with a twinkle in her eye, as if she was imparting some wisdom on the younger woman.

"But someone did take away my future." Shada told Tennis Balls about the morning's conversation with her coach and how she wouldn't be able to play for the team. "It's all I've ever wanted," she said.

"My grandson's the same way. He's still in high school, but boy does he work hard! Maybe you could get a waiver? It shouldn't be hard to prove you aren't edited."

"The leagues are hell-bent on making sports fair, even if it means some unedited humans are affected in the process."

"Still, it might be worth looking into. You never know what strings the leaders can pull."

Shada marveled at how this woman was able to see the rules as malleable, as if doors could be opened under the right circumstances. She was reminded of how different a worldview could be among people of different races—even if they were both unedited.

"I feel bad. My sister's worked to support the two of us these past few months because my big payday was on the horizon. This was supposed to be our ticket."

"I'm sure she will understand."

Shada looked at Tennis Balls with a sideways glance and ignored the comment. "I'd always wondered if I would test outside the acceptable range. Sports have always been a natural fit for me; I could run and run no matter how intense the game was. I always thought it was because of how hard I worked, but now I know it was just my genetics."

"Don't say that! Just because you were born with the ability to turn the volume up doesn't mean it gets turned up on its own. Do you think edited humans are born with all their knowledge? No, they have to learn. All the edits do is allow them to learn faster. It's not like they don't have to work, it's just that the same amount of work gets them further. Got you further, even though you aren't edited," Tennis Balls said with a wink.

The train slowed down and Shada recognized her stop. She grabbed her backpack and slung it over her shoulder. "This is me," she said.

"Good luck! Trust me, it will all work out in the end."

"Easy for you to say," Shada said as she walked off the train. Through the crowd of people she saw the apple she'd given to the homeless man, shiny and red, on the ground next to the fence alongside his tired beagle.

CHAPTER TWO

"I HAVE SOME BAD NEWS," Sikya said when Shada walked through the door of their shared apartment. She leaned on the kitchen counter with her elbows, typing on her phone.

Shada threw her backpack on the couch and plopped down next to it, grateful for the extra moment before her own bad news was spoken. She looked around their one-bedroom apartment and wondered how long Sikya would be able to afford the rent without her expected contribution. Together they kept the space spotless. The scent of lemon cleaner peaked when the kitchen was cleaned every night and lingered throughout the day. There was enough room for the couch, a coffee table, and a television in the living room, and the counter provided a barrier between it and the kitchen. The sole bathroom could be accessed from the living room or the bedroom, and unless the bathroom was in use, both doors were kept open. Their bedroom had two twin-sized beds and two dressers and left just enough space between the pieces of furniture to walk. All of it could be lost if Shada didn't find a way to help Sikya pay rent.

"What's the news?" Shada asked.

Sikya finished typing on her phone before she set the device down and laid her hands flat on the counter. She took a deep breath. "Tensen lost the election." Miles Tensen had been running for mayor and Sikya had worked on his campaign. After her sister didn't react, she launched into a tirade. "This other guy won't do a thing for the unedited, his entire campaign was paid for by WestCorp!"

"Not the first time the edited get their mayor. Hard to get past all the money."

"And legislators won't approve any limits to donations since their pockets are lined as well." Sikya looked at her phone and checked the time. "What are you doing home so early?"

Shada repositioned herself on the couch. "I got cut."

"Oh my god, I'm so sorry! Today's not a good day for us."

"We're both out of a job."

"What happened?"

"My DNA tested outside the acceptable range."

"What does that mean? Do you have to go through tryouts for a different team?"

"It means I can't play professional sports. Not just for this team, not just for this sport, but for any league in the country."

A flash of anger passed over Sikya's face. "Are you serious? Do they think you're edited?"

"They know it's natural, but the league has limits on all sorts of genetic traits."

Sikya paused for a moment. "Why don't you let me talk to Tensen for you? I'm sure he knows someone who can help."

"There's not much he can do. The leagues are separate from the government."

"But it's discrimination! We can take it to the courts."

"This is the only way leagues can make sure teams with the most money don't get an unfair advantage. Sports are the only thing unedited humans have left."

Sikya stood up and interlocked her fingers behind her head.

"I have one more paycheck coming in from the campaign, but after that we have no income. Is it time to get a job using your degree?"

Shada wanted to sulk and didn't appreciate Sikya bringing up the financial pressure they now found themselves in. "Not sure yet."

"You better become sure. One more paycheck. That's it. I've paid for everything these past few months while we waited for your first check and now it's not coming. We both have student loans, you know."

Shada sat up straight. "Now that Tensen's lost the election, you have no real reason to stay here, do you?" she asked.

"No, I guess not," Sikya said, her eyes wary.

"Coach said it's still possible to play overseas. Why don't you come with me?"

Sikya leaned her lower back against the stove. "Move overseas? I don't know if I can do that."

"Why not? It's not like we have any family left."

Sikya flinched, the memory of their mother's passing too fresh. "There's still a lot of work to do for the unedited people here. I won't stop until edits are free for everyone. It wasn't fair for mom to die because she couldn't afford to edit her DNA."

"We can go somewhere without such a divide between people."

"The divide is what I'm fighting against!"

Shada stared at Sikya. A feeling that her sister was holding back information bubbled up in her stomach. "There's more to it than what you're telling me," she said.

Sikya opened her mouth to deny the accusation then changed her mind. "I can't raise a kid overseas."

"You don't have a kid to raise."

"But I will!"

"You don't even have a man."

Sikya glared at her sister. "Not yet."

"Then let's go!"

"I told you I can't!" Sikya yelled. "There are other reasons too. My friends are here. Tensen said he will make another run at mayor, so there's lots of work to do on the campaign."

"And who's going to pay you?"

"I'm more worried about who's going to pay you."

Both sisters fell silent. Sikya was the first to speak again. "You could go and send the borrowed money back."

"You don't care if I go alone?"

"Or stay and get a job using your degree. I've supported you for months, and now I'm out of a job too. We need money from somewhere."

It was Shada's turn to glare at her sister. "You know going pro is all I ever wanted."

"Then go get paid to play!"

Shada grabbed her backpack and stormed into their shared bedroom. She pulled out her suitcase and began to throw clothes inside. One outfit each for cold and warm weather plus all the athletic clothes she might need.

"What are you doing?" Sikya asked from the doorway.

"What does it look like I'm doing?"

"Packing."

Shada stuffed a handful of underwear into the corner of her suitcase. "There, you answered your own question."

"Where are you going?"

"Overseas. You said it yourself . . . 'Go get paid to play.' So that's what I'm doing! I didn't realize I was such a burden on you. Well don't worry, I won't be much longer."

"I didn't mean go now. You don't even have a ticket."

"I can get one at the airport. I'll just charge it. I have a ton of debt already, what's a bit more?"

Sikya watched her sister finish packing and didn't say

another word until the suitcase was set down next to the front door.

Shada opened the refrigerator and took a long drink of milk before she grabbed her box of red gummy bears from the cabinet.

"I'll send your money the first chance I get," Shada said.

"Don't be like this," Sikya pleaded. "It's been a hell of a day for both of us and I didn't mean to sound like you were a burden. I'm just stressed, that's all."

"No, the message was received loud and clear. You want a return on your investment and don't want to leave. What other choice do I have than to go by myself?"

"Let's just talk to Tensen and see if he can do anything for you." Sikya walked over and placed an apple in Shada's backpack, the second apple she'd given her sister today.

Shada grabbed her bags and stood in the open doorway. "You talk to him and find out if he can help me find a team overseas who won't care about something I can't control. I'm going to the airport," she said over her shoulder before she walked through the front door without another look back.

CHAPTER THREE

SHADA'S WORLD blurred until she caught the homeless man staring at her from against the fence of the train station. She remembered the apple in her backpack she had no intention of eating and handed it to him, the second time today. The homeless man thanked her, and his small dog lifted his head and wagged his tail at Shada. She reminded herself the dog did this to everyone who paid attention to the homeless man, so she wasn't special.

It was just after noon when she boarded the train and headed back into the heart of the city. She again saw West-Corp's advertisement for financed edits, but this time she wasn't able to get the company out of her head. If the edits made her happier, the way they were supposed to, maybe she could find some contentment in a job using her degree. Her debt would double, but her life would have direction.

Shada had to switch trains in the underground hub in order to get to the airport. Flickering lights protected by translucent plastic coverings illuminated the terminal, and the brown tile floor ended at two escalators: one escalator went up and led to the airport, and one descended to the tram, which could take Shada to WestCorp's compound.

On a whim she decided to descend. She still wasn't sure whether or not she wanted to have her DNA edited, but she was curious enough to hear what the company had to say.

After she went down two more escalators she didn't know existed, Shada arrived on the platform that hosted the tram to WestCorp. It was different from the station above. It was bathed in white light thrown down from a track of lights running through the length of its center. Smooth marbled concrete benches and trash cans sat beneath the lights, the benches arranged so passengers could sit facing both directions. There was an information desk at the far end where two blond women, young but not so young they would be dismissed as uninformed, sat waiting.

Shada was the only passenger on the platform. It seemed odd to her, but she continued along the length of the platform towards the two smiling faces and asked what time the next trip would begin.

"You have twenty minutes," one of the women said. Her voice was sweet, its pitch high, and it contained a hint of amusement, as if it was engineered to sound as servile as possible.

"What brings you to WestCorp today?" her partner asked.

"I saw the ads on the train and decided to see what they are all about. Twenty minutes is a long time to wait," Shada said.

"The tram was sent as soon as you stepped onto the platform."

"It was sent for me?"

"Of course! You're the only one here."

"Where's everyone else?"

"WestCorp visitors are always scheduled in the morning. The last one left a few hours ago."

"I just came down to find out more information." Shada

looked at the light blue tiles on the wall behind the information desk arranged in a fractal pattern against a cream-colored backdrop. "Hard to believe this exists beneath the hub upstairs. Don't go through all the trouble for me, I'll just head to the airport."

"It's no trouble at all!" one of the blond women insisted.

"Really, I'll just leave." Shada turned and began to walk away.

"The tram has already been sent. Whether you stay or not doesn't affect its course."

Shada stopped. "Well, I have no place else to be . . ." she said, her voice trailing off.

"Then stay!" both women exclaimed together.

Their excitement was infectious, and Shada found herself wanting to stay in order to be around such positive energy. After the uncertainty of her day so far, it was nice to be wanted.

Shada took a seat on a smooth concrete bench and waited for the tram to arrive. She pulled out her bag of gummy bears and poured herself a handful, then ate one at a time. She found herself thinking about the two women at the information desk, about their happiness. She assumed they were edited—why else would they work on the WestCorp platform?—and if this was happiness, this cheerful disposition, was it what she could look forward to if she were to edit her DNA? Could it be worth the cost?

The tram, a single driverless car, came to a stop in front of Shada without a sound. The doors opened, Shada shouldered her backpack, and with one last look at the two women behind the information desk, who waved goodbye, she boarded the car. The tram's doors shut and the trip began as soon as Shada took a seat.

Shada was carried through a ramrod-straight tunnel and emerged on the outskirts of the city with the bay ahead. A rail extended over the water in the direction of the island on the horizon. Before the tram left land, it passed by a billboard for cologne, a square bottle surrounded by cascading water that claimed Your best you is within reach. Shada wondered how many people saw the billboard in any given week, since the edited humans of WestCorp called the island home and, to the best of her knowledge, never left.

As soon as the tram was over water, a screen descended from the ceiling. The WestCorp logo gave way to a menu, and a voice asked Shada which service she was interested in. In addition to genetic edits there were also sections for donations and business opportunities. Shada wondered what kind of donations WestCorp would be interested in and made a note to ask when she got to the island.

"Genetic edits," Shada said.

"Are you currently unedited?" the robotic voice asked.

"Yes," Shada replied. She felt strange talking to the monitor and looked around the car, grateful she was alone.

A promotional video began, showing a mother and father swinging a young child between them in a field of flowers. The video launched into the benefits of genetic editing, its safety, its efficacy, and thanked Shada for considering WestCorp, as if there was another option available for the same service. Shada couldn't help but think of Sikya and hope this small family was her sister's future.

The video ended with a note about the availability of financing options but didn't elaborate.

Shada looked out the window, to the water around her, and got the sense there was no turning back. It stirred up her rebelliousness, and she launched into a daydream about what would happen if they wouldn't accept her refusal of the genetic edits and held her hostage. What if they wouldn't provide her a ride back to the city? Would she be able to call her sister and tell her what happened? She turned around and watched the city retreat into the distance. She knew how to swim but had never done so in open water and was sure this was farther than she had ever swum before.

The tram began a gradual descent until its track ran onto the island. She passed by manicured lawns and tree-lined roads between buildings of various sizes, both residential and industrial, on her way toward the largest building: a massive square structure that looked like the largest warehouse she'd ever seen, stretching in both directions. Gleaming steel machines dotted the roof, and Shada tried to look inside one of the hundreds of windows before she plunged between two massive doors in the side of the building that opened with just enough space for the tram to pass through.

CHAPTER FOUR

SHADA DISEMBARKED from the tram onto another vacant platform. The aesthetic was the same as the one she left behind in the city except there was no information desk where she could ask for directions. The noisy sound of the bustle of crowds came down from the set of stairs situated in the same location on the platform as the escalator beneath the hub. In front of the stairs sat a security guard, the largest human Shada had ever seen, and he patted her down before he allowed her to pass. After she walked up a set of marble stairs, she emerged in the middle of a glass-covered atrium.

Rays of sunlight bisected by the glass panes spilled down onto the mass of people traveling in every direction, with Shada in the eye of the storm. Planters provided a border beneath the glass, and fernlike leaves dropped down in an effort to collect as much sunlight as possible. Sliding doors on the longest walls were separated by restaurants offering everything from coffee to seafood. Beyond the sliding doors on the corners, buses dropped off and accepted passengers. Shada assumed the four sets of drop-off points indicated that the lines of transportation made a giant X over the island.

The closest thing she could compare it to was the entrance to an airport she remembered from the one flight she'd taken with her university team for a tournament across the country.

For a moment, before she spotted a sign with an arrow in the direction of the lab, Shada debated whether or not to go back down onto the platform and head back to the city. This was her first time around so many edited people, and at first she felt like she stuck out like a sore thumb. But to her surprise, everyone went about their own business without giving her a second thought. She walked through the crowd toward the lab and looked into their eyes, searching for some way to distinguish the edited from herself. She was used to feeling out of place, a brown girl in a world made for white men, but here, to her surprise, nobody gave her a second look.

Maybe this was what set the edited humans apart.

The crowd thinned out near the entrance to the long corridor leading to the lab. Along the corridor were various displays of children's artwork, arranged by age of the artist. The quality of the work increased as the children's age increased, which corresponded to Shada's distance from the atrium. She noticed the same names multiple times and, after realizing this hall's decorations were all furnished by the same cohort, wondered if there were seventeen other corridors of similar length with other children's work on display.

The end of the corridor, another pair of sliding glass doors, came into view just before a group of a dozen or so people emerged from a door painted to match the corridor's wall on Shada's right. As the door swung closed, she spotted a bus pulling away and realized the corridor she'd just passed through was empty because everyone took the bus to different areas of the compound, even areas within walking distance. She followed the group until they went their separate ways through a series of doors arranged in a semicircle.

Shada found herself alone and stared at the unmarked doors, wondering if she should pick a door and press on into what she assumed was the entrance to the lab. The walls were stark white and the smell, a mix of chemicals and plastic, made her eyes water. She turned to go back the way she came and almost bumped into an ancient man in a white lab coat who had materialized behind her.

"Sorry," she said, her eyes downcast. She stepped to the side in an effort to let the man pass, but he didn't move.

"You're not smiling," the man said. He had a white beard, his white hair was parted to the side, and he had the kind of hunch in his upper back that gets more pronounced with age.

Shada forced her mouth into a wide grin and displayed as many teeth as she could. "Happy?" she said. In the city she would have shown the man the middle finger, but in unknown territory she didn't want to cause any trouble.

"I am. But I'm not so sure you are." He leaned in close and whispered, "You're not edited, are you?"

"No, I'm not," Shada said, sounding more proud than she intended.

"Not many unedited come to the island; most visit our office in the city. How did you make it this far into the compound?"

Shada told the man how she'd gotten off the tram, emerged into the atrium, and decided to visit the lab.

"Someone should have been waiting for you when you arrived. Plus, there's an information desk for visitors right across from the stairs. Didn't you see it?"

"No, I didn't."

"Let me show you."

The man motioned for Shada to follow him, and he shuffled in the direction of the atrium. He used his identification card to pass through the corridor doors, and the two of them stepped outside and waited under the sun. The breeze from the water cooled them off until the bus arrived. The old man's card gained him and Shada access to the driverless bus, which took them back to the atrium in a few short minutes. Back among the crowds, Shada noticed their eyes on her and heard their whispers as she was led to the information desk, right across from the stairs, right where the man in the lab coat said it would be. She felt more comfortable with the attention than when she'd walked in anonymity.

The young woman seated at the information desk hung up the phone when she saw Shada and the man in the lab coat approach. She had brunette hair, and her eyes were set deep in her face, outlined by a light shadow. When she recognized the old man, she sat up straight.

"This young lady said she got off the tram and nobody greeted her. Can you explain to me how this happened?"

The young woman flushed red. "I lost her in the crowd, sir."

"I trust you knew she was on her way. You're the one who sent the car to retrieve her, right?"

"Yes."

"Then why weren't you on the platform when she arrived?"

The young woman seemed to be weighing whether or not to explain her thought process. "It was a mistake, sir. It won't happen again."

"See that it doesn't." The man in the lab coat turned to Shada. "Enjoy your visit. And remember to smile!" he said with a satisfied grin before he walked away.

The young woman sat down behind the information desk. Shada expected her to be flustered, but her mood wasn't colored by her previous mistake. "Name?" she said in a cheerful tone Shada thought sounded artificial.

Shada got the sense this was the sort of practiced interaction she would have received if she'd approached this desk when she first walked up the stairs. "Shada Gray."

"Business at WestCorp?"

"I want information about financing genetic edits."

The young woman looked at Shada. "Are you expecting?"

"No, I came here on a whim."

"Not expected. Expecting. Pregnant."

"No, I'm not pregnant."

"So you're interested in post-birth edits?"

"Yes, that's correct."

"OK, wait here."

The young woman called for an escort, and another West-Corp employee showed up right away, as if the escort was waiting around the corner of the booth for the chance to be of service. The escort could have been the twin of one of the women at the information desk on the company's platform in the city. "Where to?" the escort asked the young woman across from Shada.

"Take her to see Alfie."

CHAPTER FIVE

SHADA WAS TAKEN up an elevator just outside the atrium and led down a hallway she guessed led to the lab. But they didn't walk far enough to be anywhere close to the lab, and when they turned off into a series of offices, Shada couldn't have found her way back without stopping to ask for directions. The labyrinth must have made sense to, or been memorized by, her escort, because there was no hesitation about which direction they took.

The escort knocked on the door of one of the offices, and a thin man sporting a gray beard and glasses, about the same height as Shada, answered. The hair on his head was also gray, and it looked as if he'd worn a baseball cap to work and taken it off when he got to the office—matted down against his head with a few thin wisps stuck out at odd angles.

"She's here to see you," the escort said before she turned around and left the two of them alone.

"Come in, come in," the gray-haired man said as he stepped back and held the door open.

Shada walked inside. The bookcases on every wall over-flowed with books, and a window in the back of the office looked out onto the water. Papers on the desk surrounded his computer, and a small picture taped onto his monitor showed a young woman. The picture was bent, and Shada guessed it had been taken many years before.

"Please sit down," the man said as he walked around the desk to his chair, gesturing to one of the two chairs across from his. "My name is Alfie Reynolds-Grant. Head scientist."

"Shada Gray."

"So you're interested in genetic edits?" Alfie said.

"Interested, yes. To be honest, I didn't think this would be such a process. I came here to find out about the financing."

"That's all you wanted? Why did they send you to me?" He sounded exasperated. "The process is straightforward. You provide an egg, we edit it, fertilize it in vitro, then transplant it into your uterus. You could've started the process in the city."

"I don't want to get pregnant. I want the edits for myself."

"Well now. That's a different story." Alfie removed his glasses, placed them in his shirt pocket, and folded his hands on his desk. "Post-birth edits are trickier, and we don't provide financing for the procedure."

Shada took a deep breath to hold back the anger bubbling inside her at having wasted so much time on this trip to the island. "Well, I can't afford the procedure otherwise. Sorry to have wasted your time." She stood up and extended her hand.

Alfie stared at her outstretched hand. "Sit down. I said we don't provide financing, not that there aren't other options available."

Shada's wary eyes didn't leave the scientist as she took a seat.

"Post-birth edits require a twenty-year contract of employment," Alfie said.

Shada's eyes widened. "Twenty years?" She swallowed hard. "That's a long time."

"It's an intensive procedure." He allowed time for the news to be digested. "Can I ask what made you decide to look into editing?"

Shada told Alfie how she'd been banned from playing in the league because her hemoglobin counts were too high. She explained how her future had boiled down to two options—either play overseas or begin a career—and how she hoped the edits would make the career more palatable.

"You already made a team?" Alfie asked. His eyes squinted as his thoughts coalesced.

"I made the team and was practicing with them when the bloodwork came back."

"Well now, this changes things." Alfie leaned back in his chair and explained how a version of this situation had occurred before. "The other guy knew his bloodwork wouldn't pass, so he got us to edit it into the acceptable range, along with the other standard edits. We agreed to provide proof that his edits had occurred before birth in exchange for him being a face for edited athletes. I won't tell you who it was or what sport he played, because he never amounted to anything more than a roster spot, but WestCorp did agree to allow his playing career to count towards his employment."

"That could be an option!" Shada said, excited to have found a solution.

"The only problem would be the failed bloodwork," Alfie said, his voice trailing off.

"I could just say I was blood doping and serve the suspension. After that, I would be free to play."

"That could work," Alfie said, nodding. "There would be approximately four months before your red blood cells could replace themselves and you would test clean. If we time it right, you could be playing professionally before the end of the year."

Shada was so excited she wanted to call her sister and share the good news, forgetting she'd stormed off a few hours before. Now she could pay Sikya back, pay off both their debts, and help Sikya pay for edits for her future children.

A potential problem occurred to Shada, and she was brought back down to earth. "One thing though," she said.

"What is it?"

"Edited players are different on the court. They always have quality technique, and should be good, but the creativity is missing. If we go through with the edits, maybe we just edit my hemoglobin count so I don't lose any of my edge."

Alfie leaned forward and rested his elbows on the desk, his chin in his hands. "Interesting. I've never considered that. Maybe that's why this didn't work the first time. In theory, we could edit you to be more creative. We've isolated the genes, and it's the same procedure."

Shada thought for a moment. "I don't think it's worth the risk. Trust me, I can be one of the greats. I just have to get on the court."

"So we would edit your hemoglobin count and say you've had the standard edits since birth, you play in the league and convince the unedited world that edits don't affect your abilities, and after your career you receive the standard edits and come work for us?"

"I would have to get the standard edits?"

"We don't allow unedited humans to work at WestCorp."

Shada sighed. "Then yes, I would get the standard edits after I retire from the league."

Alfie nodded. "I think this could work well for all parties involved." He stood up and extended his hand. "Could you come back tomorrow? I'll get this cleared with the right people and we can start the process of getting you into the league."

Alfie provided Shada with instructions on how to get back to the atrium, and Shada had to contain her excitement long enough to focus on not getting lost. On the tram back to the city —this time shared with three other passengers—she lost herself in hope. Hope for her career, hope for her future, and hope for her sister. With the money she would earn, she could pay for Sikya's living expenses and allow her sister to fight for unedited rights through legislation. It was the least she could do after her sister had allowed her to chase her own dreams these past few months.

CHAPTER SIX

SHADA STILL HAD a key to their apartment—she'd been gone as long as if she'd gone to a full day of practice—and she let herself in. Nothing had changed in the apartment other than the fact that now it was empty; Sikya must have gone out. Knowing her, it had something to do with Tensen. Maybe she was cleaning out their headquarters after the lost election or convincing voters there was still hope. Her sister came home late that night, exhausted, and found Shada on the couch watching sports news.

"What are you doing here?" Sikya asked. Surprise drained from her face and was replaced with a hesitant smile.

"I didn't go overseas," Shada said. She grabbed the remote and turned the television off.

"I see that." Sikya set her bag down on the counter. "I didn't think you would. Where'd you go?"

"I went to WestCorp."

The surprise on Sikya's face almost made Shada laugh. In a way, WestCorp was the enemy, of her and the rest of Tensen's staff. As the largest and most well-funded editors of DNA, they represented everything wrong with the state of society. Their island compound made them an easy target and provided a rallying point for those looking to advance the unedited cause.

"What were you doing there?" Sikya said, trying to sound conversational.

"I wanted to find out about financing genetic edits."

"You want to pay for edits?" Sikya asked. She leaned her shoulder against the wall outside the kitchen.

"I was on my way to the airport and there was a billboard for WestCorp that said financing is available. Come to find out it's only for pre-birth edits; post-birth edits aren't eligible."

"Headed to the airport? You really were going overseas?"

"I had every intention to when I left here earlier."

Sikya walked to the couch and sat down next to her sister. "So you went to WestCorp and found out post-birth edits aren't available for financing. I could have told you that."

"Well, I didn't know. Anyway, I got lost when I got to the island—"

"Wait, you went to the island? Why didn't you just go to their office downtown? Nobody goes to the island unless they live there and are going back."

"I didn't even know they had an office in the city. You're right, nobody goes. I was the only one on the tram."

"So you went across the water."

"I went across the water, yes. Long story short, I think I found a way to play in the league." Shada told Sikya about the plan she and Alfie had come up with, how they would edit her hemoglobin levels and claim she had been blood doping so she could serve her suspension and get back on the court before the end of the year. "He said he will come up with the paperwork saying I've been edited since birth."

Sikya's silence lasted so long Shada thought her sister would launch into a tirade when she decided to speak again. Instead, she asked, "How much will all of this cost?"

"I have to agree to work for WestCorp for twenty years. But my playing career counts towards the total. Their goal is to have an example of a successful edited athlete."

"There are plenty of edited athletes in the league."

"But none of them have been successful."

"And you will be?"

"I have a better chance at it than any edited athlete! We both know edited athletes are good but they're always missing that extra something."

Sikya continued probing Shada's plan. "And after your playing career? You just show up to work on the island?"

Shada didn't tell her sister about the plan to receive standard edits and become a cog in the WestCorp machine. "They want me to be a recruiter," she said, making up a scenario that would placate her sister. "I'd be in the city office and convince unedited couples to edit their children."

This was not the right thing to say. "You understand we'd be on different sides of the aisle, right? My whole career is dedicated to making edits free for everyone, and you'd be convincing couples to go into debt in the hopes their child has a better life. It's not fair the edited have better access to resources, including edits, when we're all members of the city, whether we live on the island or not."

"It's their choice whether they want to pay for edits or not," Shada said.

"It's their choice, but studies show most would accept the debt to edit their children if they could get approved." Sikya's voice rose in volume and she became more animated. "And do you know why they would carry that burden? Because of the pressure placed on them by the system we live in. The system I work against. And when the parents die, the debt isn't erased, it's passed down to the children!"

"Think of it this way: if I play in the league, I can afford to pay for you to live. You can devote even more time to working with Tensen for unedited equality."

"And if it comes out that my sister, who is working for West-Corp, has gone into debt for edits and pays for me to live, I'll look like a hypocrite. You just don't get it," Sikya said.

"Let people think what they want, your results will speak for themselves."

"And another thing: What's going to happen if you are successful? People will start talking. Why would you be edited at birth and I'm not? And if that's the case, why would we have grown up together?"

Shada thought for a moment. "We can say it was our parents' decision. They're both gone now, nobody could ask them and find out otherwise. Maybe they wanted to run an experiment, one edited and one unedited, and see how the situation played out."

Sikya let the suggested solution digest. "I don't know, Shada, it seems like you're signing a deal with the devil."

"What's not to know! Don't you want to edit your future child?"

Sikya sighed and lowered her head. "Yes, but I want to be able to afford it. I'm not going into more debt, nor will I risk putting my child into debt, just for edits."

"If I play in the league, we will be able to afford it!"

Sikya looked at Shada with tears in her eyes. "Don't do this just for me and a child that doesn't exist yet."

"I'm doing this for us."

"And you'll still be the same, right? You're just getting edits to get your hemoglobin count in the proper range and not the standard edits?"

Shada couldn't remember a time when she'd outright lied to her sister, but she was so close to receiving her sister's blessing she had to press on. "Just the edits so I can play in the league." At first.

"OK," Sikya said with an exhale. She leaned in and gave her sister a hug. "I'm glad you didn't make it to the airport."

"Me too," Shada said as she caught the scent of the city in Sikya's hair.

CHAPTER SEVEN

SHADA WAITED on the platform to be taken to WestCorp's island compound during rush hour the next morning. There were, she guessed, about forty people there with her, enough that all the concrete benches were taken and the remaining individuals had to stand until transportation arrived. They came from all walks of life: older individuals dressed in business attire stood alongside young adults who looked like they were on their way to the gym. Shada was dressed somewhere in between, having borrowed some of her sister's clothes after Sikya insisted she not wear her normal gym shorts and T-shirt. Sikya had decided on a pair of black pants and a black blouse for Shada but couldn't convince her sister to wear anything but sneakers.

Two women were at the information desk when Shada arrived. None of the commuters bothered to approach them, and they talked to each other with broad smiles, white teeth on full display. From a distance they looked to be the same two women Shada had interacted with the day before, but she never got close enough to be sure. What could they be talking about if they saw each other every day? She imagined she would talk about sports if she was in their position, since there was always news about some team somewhere. Maybe they agreed on which television shows they watched just so they would have something to talk about.

The tram arrived with three cars, enough to accommodate all the travelers. The cars were dark as they pulled up, but a soft white light blinked on the second the vehicle stopped, spilling out onto the mass of people lined up in front of six opening doors. Everyone filed into the tram and found seats. Shada ended up next to a young woman, about her age, with a septum piercing and plenty of metal on the lobes of each ear. Shada's neighbor asked her why she was going to WestCorp as the tram began to move.

"Edits," she murmured, not sure if the woman next to her was edited or not. There was still something about edited humans Shada mistrusted, since they grew up and lived in a different world from hers, and she felt like she was about to enter a beehive full of people who could sting her if provoked. She wondered if Sikya's attitude about the edited taking advantage of the unedited had rubbed off on her.

"Me too," the pierced woman said, nodding. "I'm not pregnant though, nor do I want to be. These are for me." From the sound of it, the woman had made peace with her decision.

"I'm going in for post-birth edits too," Shada said. She kept her statement vague on purpose, hopeful this woman would assume they were the standard edits so she wouldn't have to elaborate.

Shada wondered what the odds were that she'd ended up next to another unedited heading to the island for post-birth edits. From the way Alfie had made it sound, the procedure wasn't as straightforward as the pre-birth edits, and she got the sense it was out of the ordinary. She glanced around the car at the same moment the tram left the underground tunnel, wondering if perhaps all the people whose faces had just been illuminated by sunlight were on their way to the island for the same reason as them. Since she knew there was no discernible difference in structure between the two types of humans, she gave up and turned to watch the island materialize on the horizon, thinking that perhaps everyone on board assumed they were the only unedited human making this morning's commute.

Shada's pierced neighbor laughed at the billboard for cologne they passed before crossing the water. "Nothing could mask the stench of this city," she said. She tucked her chin, turned in Shada's direction, and looked at her fellow passenger through the sides of her eyes. She held out her right hand. "My name's Chloe."

They shook hands. "Shada Gray."

"My name's Chloe Rose."

Her eyes were a blue so faint they could have been white if seen at a glance. Shada wondered if this was her natural eye color.

"Did you meet with Alfie?" Shada asked.

"Who?"

"The head scientist on the island. I came yesterday and sat down with him. He told me to come back today."

Chloe looked at Shada with wide eyes. "You've already been to the island?"

Shada nodded.

"I went to the WestCorp office in the city last week and they set it up for me to come today. I went in to find out about the employment after the edits," Chloe said. She turned forward as the tram continued its trip over the water. "I just got tired of the rat race, you know?"

Shada furrowed her brow. "You want employment even though you're tired of the rat race?" She was surprised at herself for calling out the apparent contradiction; any other time she would have taken note of the discrepancy and left it alone. She was reminded of Sikya, who never let someone off the hook for misaligned statements.

"I've accepted that the rat race is a part of life, but I just don't want to be tired of it anymore. If the edits can make me happy with a lifetime of work, then why not invest in myself?"

Shada took a moment to ponder Chloe's position and recognized the similarity within herself. Her own decision hadn't arrived with such a succinct awareness of motivation, but she recognized the logic.

"Twenty years is a long time," Shada said, both to Chloe and as a reminder to herself. This wasn't a second guess of her decision, just a statement of fact.

"And we're both looking at it. Maybe we can work together!" Chloe said.

"Maybe," Shada said, knowing the beginning of her West-Corp career wouldn't be with Chloe. "I'm not sure how they decide where we work. They just told me that I had to work for WestCorp."

"That's all they told me too. But maybe, if we ask, they can set it up. Even if we aren't good at the same stuff now, they could edit us to be good fits for the same position, right?"

Shada had never considered whether there was any specialization implied with the edits. She assumed the edits were the same for everyone and allowed everyone to succeed wherever they were assigned. Did the edited still have people who were better at math, or art, the way unedited humans did? The difference in quality of artwork in the corridor led Shada to believe such differences existed, but she wasn't sure if the differences survived into adulthood. Maybe edited children all grew up into a shared skill set, but recipients of post-birth edits wouldn't reach the same position since they weren't trained in the same fashion..

"It'd be nice to have a familiar face to work with. Not sure if

I want to see you for twenty years though!" Shada said with a laugh.

Chloe laughed too. "If we're edited to be happy then it won't matter. The time will fly by!"

Out of the corner of her eye, Shada saw the smile evaporate from Chloe's face, as if she didn't have the strength or desire to sustain the expression.

The tram descended onto the island, and both women stared out the window as the greenery flew by. After growing up in the city, a mass of steel and concrete, the onslaught of green was enough to kill their conversation until they arrived beneath the atrium.

"Let's get this over with," Chloe said as the doors opened.

CHAPTER EIGHT

Two massive guards at the foot of the stairs—where one had sat yesterday—patted down each visitor before they were allowed to ascend into the atrium. Chloe, after passing through security first, waited for Shada before they walked up the stairs together. They arrived in the atrium and both stared at the sea of edited humans passing by in every direction as their fellow passengers came up the stairs, walked past them, and joined the chaos.

Shada grabbed Chloe's arm and began to lead her to the information desk she had been shown to the day before. She expected to see the same young woman, but this time a young man sat in her place.

"Shada Gray and Chloe Rose," a female voice yelled from behind them.

Shada released Chloe, they both turned around, and Shada watched a young woman with dark red hair walk towards them with a clipboard in hand and scowl on her face. "I see you found each other," the WestCorp employee said.

"We did," Chloe said.

Shada wondered if WestCorp had somehow made sure they

met each other, but she couldn't see how it would have been done. Odds were it was dumb luck that drew them to each other —that, or a sort of unedited magnetism unknown to either of them. And what if they had come up the stairs and walked in different directions? Would this woman have had to wrangle them out of the crowd before they ended up somewhere they weren't supposed to be?

"My name is Piper Lawson. Please follow me."

For some reason Shada expected to follow the woman to Alfie's office, or to the lab, but instead they boarded a bus on the opposite side of the atrium. The clouds overhead blocked the sunlight from beaming down on them, but it was still hot enough for beads of sweat to gather on both Shada's and Chloe's foreheads. Piper didn't seem to be affected by the heat.

Nobody made any attempts at small talk, and after a five-minute bus ride they pulled up next to a warehouse. The bus stop was shaded by palm trees, and thin strips of grass lined the front of the building. They were led inside and met by a sea of stainless steel examining tables with fresh white pillows on each.

"What are all these tables for?" Chloe asked.

"Post-birth edits," Piper said from ahead of them. She couldn't have been more dismissive.

Chloe and Shada looked at each other. It was just the two of them, as far as either of them could tell, and they didn't see why so many tables would ever be needed.

Piper must have sensed their confusion because she sighed before elaborating. "We schedule post-birth edits to occur on the same day and knock them out all at once. You two were chosen to participate in a separate procedure."

"Nobody said anything about a separate procedure," Chloe said, crossing her arms.

"You'll find out more in a moment. If you decide this procedure isn't right for you, we will have you come back when the rest of the post-birth edits occur, next Monday. Of course, you'll be compensated for your time today."

"Next Monday? I don't want to waste any more time. I've waited almost a month for this already!" Chloe said.

Shada was surprised to hear how long it had taken Chloe; it had only been a day since she first decided to investigate edits. She knew she was lucky the process took so little time, so she didn't bring up her own objections even though she wanted to get back in the league as soon as possible.

"If you've waited a month, then what's a few days more?" Piper asked as they reached their destination, a room with glass windows at the end of the warehouse. "Please take a seat inside," Piper said before Chloe had a chance to say another word.

There were two tables surrounded by six chairs each and a projector screen on one wall. The rest of the room was bare. Piper pulled out her phone, larger than most, and tapped it a few times before the projector came to life. She shut the blinds before taking her seat. "Before we continue, I must urge your discretion. But even if you were to tell someone, they wouldn't believe you."

"What choice do we have?" Shada said.

"There's always a choice," Piper countered.

"Play the damn thing," Chloe said.

Shada nodded.

Piper pressed play on a series of videos. The footage was raw and looked as if it had been shot during experiments in a facility similar to the one they were in. First, they watched as test subjects learned to control virtual avatars with their minds. Then, test subjects' consciousnesses were shown to be uploaded into lizards, rats, small dogs, then monkeys. Each time, a series of tests was conducted that showed the animals answering a series of questions about math and pop culture by walking onto circles with the correct answer.

Chloe and Shada were watching WestCorp's development of uploaded consciousness.

The last video showed the upload of a man in a white lab coat into a human. Instead of answering questions by stepping onto the correct answer, the human test subject demonstrated fine motor control by conducting a chemical experiment that proved the unconscious man in the white lab coat, in the background, was in control of the host through the wires attached to both skulls. When the upload was reversed, the man in the white lab coat sat up. "It worked," he said through bloodshot eyes.

Shada recognized Alfie, ten years younger, and the reason why she was in the room with Chloe solidified. "They want to control our bodies?" she asked.

"The last footage was simple control of the body, yes. Its original design was for experts to enter dangerous environments without placing themselves in harm's way. Think astronauts entering space with years of specialized training without their physical bodies being put in jeopardy."

"You created people to be sacrificed," Chloe said, her mouth open.

"Don't you see the benefits? With a simple connection it was possible to gain control of limbs much more precisely than any robot could. Paralyzed humans could walk again. Though there was a surprise once the connection no longer had to be hardwired."

"What was the surprise?" Shada asked.

"The uploaded consciousness was able to feel whatever the human host felt. Fear, anxiety, love . . . it led to some less-than-desirable results."

"Like what?" Chloe asked.

"An expert miner felt what it was like to die when his host got caught in a collapse. It drove him crazy."

"Good," Shada said. She wasn't comfortable with what she was being shown and felt like whoever uploaded their mind deserved what they had coming to them.

"We realized the applications we envisioned had to be revisited." The slideshow had ended, and the projector now clicked into standby mode.

"And this is where we come in," said Chloe.

Piper ignored her. "Since emotions could be felt, and the edited humans no longer had the coping mechanisms to deal with the emotions, there couldn't be any situations that would generate a negative response."

"So only good feelings," Chloe said.

Piper glared at Chloe. "In a way. This is still under development, but right now we allow senior WestCorp officials to pay willing participants in order to explore what emotions feel like, since theirs have been edited to be stable at all times."

Shada remembered the screen on the tram had an option for donations and wondered if this was what was meant.

"There are other applications being explored, but this is why you have been brought here apart from the others: to find out if you'd be willing to be paid in order to allow edited humans access to your emotions for one to two hours."

Shada didn't know how she felt about letting her body be used this way, but Chloe sat up and said that as long as the price was right, they could do whatever they wanted.

"What's stopping them from taking over permanently?" Shada whispered, more to herself than to anyone else, but the other two women fell silent.

"We work with a group of unedited humans who register the time you will be taken over and ensure your return."

"How would they know we weren't hijacked permanently?" Chloe said.

Piper winced at the word hijacked but answered the question. "There's an interview, and a series of questions, that only you would know the answers to. As long as you deem the safety check satisfactory, we could upload a consciousness by the end of the week."

"So . . . we agree, get placed on a list, and wait until someone chooses to take us for a spin?" Chloe said.

"No, you've already been chosen. You just have to agree," Piper said.

CHAPTER NINE

SHADA AND CHLOE traveled from the island to the financial district of the city to meet with officials in the Office of Unedited Rights before they gave Piper their final answer. Because of Sikya, Shada knew Miles Tensen had worked here before he made a run for mayor, and she wondered if he'd come back to the same job after he lost the election.

Chloe, Shada knew from their discussion on the trip back to the city, was leaning towards allowing someone to hijack her body. She planned to set aside the money for her retirement, when she no longer had to work and could live outside the city on a farm, away from everyone. When Shada asked why she would want to retire when she would, in theory, be happy working at WestCorp, Chloe replied that she hoped to make enough money to buy the house before she was edited. It would cement her plan for after the twenty years were up, regardless of how she felt at the time.

Shada was surprised Chloe had given her pre-edit decisions so much weight. She herself leaned towards allowing the hijacking as well, but for different reasons. She told Chloe the opportunity was a way to pay back the money she owed her sister, and if possible, pay off both their student debt. What she didn't mention was that if she could go into the league back at financial zero, she would be able to enjoy playing the sport she loved without worrying about money.

The light brown stone of the building Piper had directed them to visit loomed over them, and honking cars sat in its shadow, the evening traffic making movement tedious. Brown marble floors and chandeliers greeted Shada when she passed through the revolving doors. The security guards were dressed in white and wore white-rimmed glasses. Chloe and Shada got into the elevator and rode it to the seventeenth floor. The Office of Unedited Rights was on a corner of the building and had floor-to-ceiling windows overlooking the city. A young Asian man wearing a blue suit and white-rimmed glasses, the same style as the guards below, sat at the reception desk and greeted them when they walked inside.

"How can I help you today?" he asked with a confident smile.

Shada wasn't sure how much information to divulge but didn't have to worry, because Chloe answered for both of them. "WestCorp sent us over before we get hijacked," she said.

A cloud passed over the man's face and blocked the shine of his smile before he regained his composure. Shada couldn't decide if the darkness was pity or the look of a man betrayed. "Of course, we were told to expect you. Please take a seat. Mr. Tensen will see you in a moment."

After they were both seated, Shada whispered to Chloe that Tensen had lost the mayoral election a few days ago and that her sister had worked on his campaign.

"Does she work here?" Chloe said, looking around the office.

"No, she worked for him outside, at election headquarters. Maybe now that the campaign is over she will try and get a job in here, but I haven't talked to her about it and don't know for sure."

"She should try. You see how nice this building is? I bet they make good money here." She used her chin to point to the various desks in the offices visible from where they sat.

"I'm sure they do. I'll suggest it." Shada didn't have any intention of telling Sikya about WestCorp's offer to hijack her body, knowing her sister wouldn't approve. She wondered how she would explain her reason for meeting with Tensen without divulging more than her sister needed to know. Plus, if her sister ever worked here, would she have access to Shada's file? This wasn't something Shada wanted Sikya to find out without her around to explain.

The secretary told "Ms. Gray" that Mr. Tensen was ready to see her.

"Good luck," Chloe said as she leaned back in her chair, laid her head against the wall, and closed her eyes.

Mr. Tensen stood behind his desk when Shada entered the room. After introductions, Shada told him her sister worked on his campaign.

"I can see the resemblance," Tensen said as he took a seat. He was handsome, his black hair parted on the side, and his square jaw emanated a strength tempered by his kind eyes. If Shada had seen Sikya on the street next to this man, she would assume her sister would want to have his child. Even now, knowing their relationship was professional and never having heard Sikya say anything to make her think otherwise, she wondered if Sikya didn't harbor romantic feelings.

"Let me tell you how this is going to work," Tensen began. "We need to come up with a standard confirmation of identity screen. It's mostly stuff from your childhood, things nobody could quantify and search for. After we go through the questions—there are about fifty total—I can answer any questions you may have."

The questions ranged from first crushes to childhood injuries to favorite foods and vacations. Tensen encouraged Shada to elaborate on each, to tell stories about all of them, so that there would be more data to analyze in the event confirmation was required.

As soon as Tensen was finished, Shada began asking the questions she had saved up. "First, how would anyone know to put this test to use? If whoever hijacks my body takes over, couldn't they just pretend to be me and take over my life?"

Tensen nodded. "Good question. Before you undergo the procedure, you let us know the exact times you will be unreachable."

Shada appreciated the euphemism.

"Once the predetermined time is over, we administer a quick confirmation via telephone. We've never had to administer the full confirmation, but to prevent a permanent takeover, we ask that you call in three days later for a second confirmation. Now, if for some reason you are unreachable and we don't find out because whoever has control passes these two tests, we have one final fail-safe. One week after the procedure ends, we call a person of your choosing, someone who knows you well, and tell them we are your therapist checking in on you. We ask if they have noticed anything strange in your behavior or if you have acted differently. If, for whatever reason, they say yes, we administer the full confirmation."

Shada nodded, knowing Sikya would be the person they would contact and grateful they had a cover story already set up. She knew Sikya would appreciate the fact she had a therapist and wouldn't ask too many questions. "And if the confirmation test fails? What then?"

"The authorities will become involved. By law, WestCorp is

required to allow them access to their files. Between you and me, WestCorp doesn't want anyone snooping around their files, so they have no reason to violate the terms."

"The authorities? Which authorities can control WestCorp?"

"They use the procedure as well. Have you ever heard of someone receiving multiple life sentences? Well, those years are accrued by implanting their consciousness into members of death row. Nobody, or should I say no body, has been put to death for a number of years now. Whoever receives a death sentence becomes a vessel for another consciousness who is forced to serve their sentence."

Shada shuddered. "What happens to the consciousness of the vessel?"

"The consciousness of the inmate sentenced to death is forced into the background."

"They're trapped?"

"In a sense. Life imprisonment is less than the death penalty, so in a way, they are having their sentence reduced."

"Or made worse, since their mind is now imprisoned as well."

"I guess it depends on how you look at it."

Shada nodded, not sure of how she herself looked at it.

"Now, who should we contact a week after your procedure?"

Shada told Tensen to contact Sikya and gave him her contact information. Tensen nodded as if he already knew this information but was being issued a reminder.

"OK, you're all set!" Tensen said, leaning back in his chair.

Shada looked at the clock on his wall. Their discussion had lasted a little over half an hour.

"Do you have any other questions?" Tensen said.

Shada looked up and took a breath. "I don't think so . . ."

"Well, if you think of anything, just give our office a call." Tensen stood up and shook hands with Shada. "It was nice to meet you after working with your sister during the campaign," he said.

"Nice meeting you too. I was sorry to hear you lost."

"Me too," he said, his eyes lowering. After a moment he looked up. "Could you please tell Ms. Rose to come in?"

CHAPTER TEN

BOTH CHLOE AND SHADA, convinced Tensen's protection against permanent takeover would take care of them in a worst-case scenario, traveled to the island of the edited the next afternoon. Piper asked them to sit together under the glass ceiling of the atrium and provided them both with credits that could be used at any of the scattered restaurants before she walked away, telling them she would be back. Instead of a typical lunch, Shada bought herself a fruit platter and a smoothie; Chloe got a muffin and a coffee.

"Do you think it will hurt?" Chloe asked Shada with food still in her mouth. A few crumbs fell onto her shirt.

"The procedure? Not sure. I'm curious where I'm supposed to go when I'm no longer in control . . . think it's like falling asleep?" Shada asked. She plopped a piece of melon into her mouth, cut larger than she'd prefer but too small to be taken in two bites.

"Maybe it's like sleepwalking, since whoever is in control will want to walk around and experience stuff."

Shada nodded, unsure if Chloe was as nervous as she was. She stared at the faces of the people walking by and tried to determine if any of them were the ones interested in hijacking her body.

"I wonder how they're going to deal with my anxiety," Chloe said into the silence that had fallen between them.

"What do you mean?"

"I've had anxiety my entire life. I'm used to dealing with it, but an edited person . . . I can't imagine they've ever felt anything like it."

"Piper said the experiences are made to be positive. Puppies and rainbows. No room for anxiety."

Chloe shook her head. "So you've never had anxiety," she said with a chuckle. She took a long drink of her coffee.

"Doesn't it burn your tongue?" Shada asked.

"I always drink it hot," Chloe responded. Her eyes were pulled to something behind Shada.

Shada turned around and saw Piper approach their table, back from wherever she had gone.

"Come with me," Piper said.

Piper led them in the direction of the lab, but instead of walking down the long corridor, she went through a door on the corridor's left and led them to a waiting bus. The bus took them in a straight line to what Shada knew was the end of the corridor, they got off, and Piper swiped her identification card to get into the lab.

"Do these procedures ever become sexual?" Chloe said to Piper's back.

"Sexual? Not with you," Piper sneered without turning around. "Edited humans only have sex with other edited humans. We have no desire to get caught up with the unedited's never-ending drive to procreate. It's part of what keeps us happier than the unedited."

"Sex with your neighbors makes you happier?" Chloe asked.

She looked at Shada with one eyebrow raised, asking wordlessly if the woman ahead of them was crazy.

"The lack of a bio-clock means we only need to replace ourselves. One boy and one girl. Each parent is responsible for raising the opposite gender in order to maintain the gender neutrality on the island."

Shada mentioned that she hadn't seen any children. "Other than their artwork," she said.

"They're on a different part of the island, with the older members of WestCorp. When we are younger we stay focused on our work, and it's only when our physical stamina decreases that we are responsible for raising offspring. The two who want to upload into your bodies no longer have children to raise and are interested in more abstract matters now that they have so much time available to them in their twilight years."

Piper led them into a side hallway, and Chloe was told to wait in one room while Shada was led into the one adjacent.

The room was small, cold, and had just enough room for two stainless steel tables and a collection of wires connected to a monitor between them.

"Take a seat on this one," Piper said, tapping the table farthest away from the door. "Alfie will be in here in a minute," she said before she walked out.

Shada sat down, and a few minutes later Alfie walked in.

"Good morning," he said. He set a manila folder on the second table and began flipping through sheets of loose paper. His gray hair was combed flat, and his white lab coat had been pressed; straight lines ran down each side. The top of his blue button-down, the top button unbuttoned, showed above the lab coat, and a pair of dark brown wing tips sat beneath khaki pants with a slight break.

"Mornin'," Shada said.

"You need to sign a few documents."

Alfie handed Shada a packet of paper. "This one says you spoke with the Office of Unedited Rights."

Shada hopped off the table and used its surface to initial the bottom of each page and sign the last. She was handed another.

"And this one says you are aware of the procedure you are about to undergo."

Again Shada signed, then Alfie took the packet back and replaced it with a third.

"Last one; this one says you agree to a two-hour time limit."

Shada signed then handed the pages back to Alfie. "Do I get to meet the person who wants to take over my body?" she asked.

"Under normal circumstances, no, we keep the uploader anonymous. But this person has informed me the two of you have already met." Alfie double-checked the paperwork and closed the manila folder. "He asked to meet you before the upload. Of course, when he asks, he really means he wants it done."

"I've already met him?" Shada asked.

"You have. He's the head of WestCorp."

Shada felt her stomach drop, as if the ground had been pulled away and she was in freefall.

"The head of WestCorp wants to take my body for a ride? When would I have met him?" Shada said, her voice trailing off.

The door opened, and the old man who'd found Shada walking around the lab on her first visit walked in. Alfie introduced him. "Shada, this is Michael Hollis."

The hunched man with the white beard wore a black T-shirt tucked into black sweatpants. No lab coat this time. "Hello, Shada," he said with a wrinkled smile.

They shook hands. "It's nice to officially meet you," he said.

Shada stared at his face for a moment before she remembered her manners. "Likewise," she said. She made sure not to smile.

"I hope this request wasn't too much," Hollis said.

"Is this your first time being uploaded?" Shada asked.

Alfie and Hollis shared a laugh. "No, we've done this before."

"But never anyone with your athletic pedigree. I'm hoping to feel what it's like to run again, to jump again, to move again." Hollis looked down at his age-spotted hands. "This body has been breaking down for years," he said with disgust. "I started WestCorp when I was young and ignored my body. Now I'm in a position where I can pay for a visit to what could have been if I had been born to different parents."

Shada was surprised to hear that both she and Hollis, opposites in almost every measurable aspect, wondered what life was like on the other side.

Alfie removed his folder from the table and instructed Hollis to lie down. He placed a modified helmet covered with strings of lights over the old man's head before he turned to Shada and motioned for her to lie down as well.

"Does Chloe have to wait until we are through before she gets hijacked?" Shada asked.

"A member of my research team should be over there right now getting her set up. There's a screen between the tables in her room, so she won't find out who takes control."

Shada noticed a thin door in the wall opposite the monitor apparatus where the screen must be kept.

"Hollis is the only person I upload myself," Alfie said. He secured the modified helmet on her head. "You'll feel a tingling sensation before Hollis takes over. Some people report being able to sense the switch through darkness, and some say it feels like they were asleep the whole time. Your body, with Hollis in control, will go through a series of exercises handpicked by Hollis."

"Will Chloe be there too?"

"No, the only person you—or should I say, your body—will come into contact with is me. She will be led to a different area of the compound for a standard visit."

"Filled with puppies and rainbows?"

Alfie laughed. "Something like that. Are you ready?"

"Ready as I'll ever be," both Hollis and Shada said at the same time.

CHAPTER ELEVEN

SHADA GOT the sense the world was a television show and her eyes were the screen. The signal was weak at first; her surroundings were blurred, and she wasn't able to distinguish anything other than the difference between light and dark. A swell of panic arose from somewhere not inside herself—because the connection to her body had been severed—but from the belief she should be panicked. Without the associated feelings, her mind became frantic. In an effort to distill her thoughts using language, she tried to label the situation and settled on "sleep paralysis," though she had never experienced it before. What else could she call the disconnection of her external experiences with her internal dialogue?

Disconnection. She remembered being connected to the machine through the helmet, then . . . nothing. Where did she go, and where was she now? She couldn't feel her body but tried to take ten breaths anyway with the hope of latching onto something, anything. She wasn't able to find air, but the act of counting to ten calmed her mind and allowed the world to come into greater focus.

Shada watched herself be led outside and into the sun by

Alfie. The brightness outside must have affected her body, or its user, because a hand was lifted over her eyes through no effort of her own. She knew someone else was in control but couldn't place the identity of who it might be. It felt like the name was on the tip of her tongue and she could discover the name if she could just regain control.

Her body turned and watched Alfie pick up a frisbee. Shada had never played with one before but knew their purpose. Alfie waited for Shada's body to back up before he tossed the toy. It flew through the air, a white disk against a blue backdrop, before a hand appeared from Shada's periphery and snagged it from the air.

"She's got good reflexes," Shada heard herself say. Up until this point, she hadn't heard anything at all.

"Lifelong athlete," Alfie shouted back.

Shada's body threw the frisbee back to Alfie. The two of them tossed the toy back and forth while Shada groped for a sensation, any sensation, to ground herself with. It was like she was floating in space after being cut from a spaceship, with no gravity to pull her down. Except instead of her body it was her thoughts that had become untethered.

Another count to ten without registering the sensation of breath and she remembered who had control of her body. Hollis, the old man. She assumed he was still back on the table in the small room, unconscious, his body kept alive for no real reason since his mind had abandoned it.

Shada witnessed her attention turn towards a large tire on the grass by the wall of the warehouse. She watched the tire get closer and witnessed herself flip it over. Three flips later and Hollis must have decided he'd had enough, because Shada's body sprinted away through the grass. When he turned her body around and looked at Alfie, the lead scientist smiled as if mirroring Shada's expression.

"Let's see how high she can jump," Shada heard herself say.

Shada's arm reached up high against the wall. Alfie, who had jogged up to come up alongside her, said he would keep an eye on where she reached. Her body jumped and touched as high as possible, but Shada thought she could get higher if she was in control.

"Six bricks," Alfie said.

"See how high you can touch," Hollis-in-Shada commanded Alfie.

Alfie lined himself up against the wall, measured his reach, then jumped, and was able to touch three bricks higher than the one he'd first touched.

"This woman's got some springs," Shada's voice rang out.

After a few more exercises, including an attempt at a handstand, which almost broke Shada's neck but for which she felt nothing, Hollis said he wanted to go to the animal testing building.

"Sir, that's going to be a problem."

Shada saw the world sideways as her head tilted. "Why?"

"Unedited humans get distressed when they see animals, particularly dogs, being tested on. Since you're edited, you don't have the ability to cope with the negative emotions that might arise. Also, the trip there and back would put us too close to the two-hour limit."

"Damnit, Alfie, you're wasting our time by talking so much! Take me there, I can pay her more if we run over. I'm sure she won't mind the extra money."

Alfie shook his head and waved for a small private vehicle to pick them up, unseen by Shada until Hollis turned her head to watch its approach.

Shada was disgusted as her body walked between cages of dogs stacked three high and arranged into long aisles. Some dogs had limbs too small for their bodies, some too large, and some had fur in various stages of mange. She had no awareness of the typical feelings associated with disgust, just the sense she would be disgusted if she was in control of herself.

"What do you feel?" Alfie asked.

"Shortness of breath, tension in the abdominal cavity, a desire to help . . . is this what unedited humans deal with every day?" Shada's voice answered.

"Not every day, just when certain conditions are met."

"I can't control my breath," Hollis-in-Shada said. Shada believed she heard a trace of panic in her voice but couldn't be sure. The dogs stared at Shada with sad eyes, as if they could sense someone was among them who could recognize their plight.

"Her breaths are shallow and fast. Try and slow them down, take big breaths. Closing your eyes might help."

Shada lost her view of the world but could hear herself taking big gulps of air. She focused on the sound and was able to feel herself take a breath, the first sensation she'd felt since control of her body was taken from her. She latched on to the action with long tendrils of awareness but wasn't able to exert any control. A dog barked, and Hollis opened her eyes, ending the spell.

"Let's get out of here," Hollis said in Shada's voice.

"We never should have come."

They rushed back outside and Hollis, in Shada's body, grabbed hold of a tree and pressed his cheek against its bark. He closed her eyes and took a series of breaths unreachable by Shada while she, trapped inside her own body, waited for the edited man to come to terms with the way sadness felt.

"Let's go," Alfie said.

Hollis opened Shada's eyes and she saw Alfie next to her, one arm around her shoulder. Alfie led Hollis-in-Shada to the private vehicle and back to the room where the upload took place.

"Just in time," Alfie said, looking at his watch.

"See, it all worked out," Hollis-in-Shada said without much conviction.

When Shada woke up, aware of her body once more, she took ten grateful breaths through her nose before she opened her eyes. She sat up and looked at the empty table next to her. Alfie was writing on a paper inside the manila folder.

"Where's Hollis?"

"He had urgent business to attend to." Alfie shut the folder and turned to Shada. "How do you feel?"

Part of her wanted to bring up the animal testing she'd witnessed, but the effect it might have on her future payday held her tongue. "Hungry," she said.

Alfie pulled a bag of gummies from his pocket. "Eat these; your body did a lot of exercise, and the sugar will help take the edge off."

Shada ate the red ones and left the rest in the packet. Her phone rang, her identity was confirmed, and after Chloe, who said she'd felt like she was asleep the entire time, met them in the hall outside their respective rooms, Alfie led them both back to the atrium. He was able to inform them their payment would be in their accounts by the time they got back to the city before Piper showed up, whispered something into his ear, and they both rushed away.

CHAPTER TWELVE

WHEN SHADA GAVE her sister the money she owed, and the money for the next few months' rent, Sikya asked how the money had already arrived. They were together in their apartment—the apartment Sikya had paid for over the last few months—Shada on the couch and Sikya leaning against the doorframe of their room.

"You didn't tell me you signed the contract!" Sikya said, excited.

"The money isn't from the team, it's from WestCorp," Shada said. Any apprehension about her sister's attitude toward the procedure had evaporated the second Shada got home and realized how tired she was. Both she and Chloe had stared straight ahead for the entirety of the trip back to the city from the island, and when they parted ways, neither of them bothered to say goodbye to the other. They weren't able to address the exhaustion of the other in case language magnified the feeling in themselves.

Sikya, to Shada's surprise, responded with confusion. "WestCorp paid you? Aren't they the ones who are supposed to get paid? That's why you have to work for them after your playing career."

Shada explained how she had been offered enough money to pay Sikya back and take a sizable chunk from her loans in order let someone take control of her body for two hours.

"You did what?" Sikya screamed at Shada, her eyes wide open.

"Allowed them to control my body," Shada said, her patience wearing thin. "There were two tables, I had to put on a weird helmet, and then someone's mind was uploaded into my body."

Sikya paced the length of the living room. "I can't believe you let yourself be used like that," she said, upset. Sadness, rather than anger, emanated from her frown.

"It wasn't terrible. And the money's good so I don't regret it."

"What was it like?"

Shada didn't want to go into specifics about the experience of watching the world through her own eyes without the associated sensations, so she used Chloe's experience to describe the procedure to her sister. "I fell asleep, and two hours later I woke up. I never saw the person who took over, there was a screen between our tables, and they were gone when I woke up."

"What if some pervert wanted to take control of your body? They could have used you for their sick fetish!"

"It's not like that. The people who pay to be uploaded want to feel what it's like to be unedited. My body was taken through a series of experiences designed to generate positive feelings," Shada said. She thought she sounded like one of the informative videos WestCorp made. "Edited humans don't have the coping mechanisms in place to deal with negative emotions, so it's all puppies and rainbows."

"Sex can be a positive feeling."

"It can be, yes, but that's not the point."

"How do you know?"

Shada told her sister about Piper's explanation of the edited's attitude towards sex and reproduction, including the way Piper looked down on the unedited.

"What if this is their last chance to get their freak on after a lifetime of only having sex with edited people? I don't like this at all. There are other ways to make money!"

"This much this quick? I don't see how. Trust me, they want nothing to do with me sexually."

"Was this a onetime thing?" Sikya said, a flash of protective anger passing over her face.

Shada winced at the thought of going through the experience again. "Nobody mentioned a next time, but if it was offered, I don't see why not. We can use the money."

Sikya shook her head, angry and defeated. She sat down on the couch next to Shada. "This has been one hell of a day," she said, exasperated.

"What happened with you?" Shada asked.

"Tensen told me he can't get me a job at the office he works at. He's offered to keep me as part of his campaign team for the next election, but he won't be able to pay me anywhere close to what I was making."

Shada decided it wasn't the right time to tell her sister about her visit to the Office of Unedited Rights to meet with Tensen. "Then I should try and undergo the procedure again! And if there's this much money involved, I could pay for you to get edited without taking on more debt."

If Shada had slapped Sikya across the face, her sister couldn't have been caught more off guard. "I will never get edited," she snarled.

"You say it like it's the worst thing in the world. Don't you want to have an edited child?"

"About that . . . I'm not sure I can even have a child. I put in an application for a birth license and found out today it's been denied."

"You put one in by yourself? No wonder you were denied. If every person who wanted a kid just went out and had one, there would be no way the city could sustain itself."

"I was making good money and decided to see if they would allow it." Sikya leaned her head back on the couch's top cushion and closed her eyes.

"Without someone else, the financials don't work out. How about you put me down as a co-parent once I sign the contract with the league? There should be enough income between the two of us to afford it."

"Same-sex couples aren't a problem, but I don't know if they would let siblings raise a child."

"Well, once money starts coming in, we could try. Plus, I could afford to edit the child. The WestCorp bump should be good enough to get you a license."

Sikya paused. "I don't want to edit them anymore," she pronounced.

Shada turned to look at her sister and saw Sikya stare at her down the length of her nose. Sikya sat up, and they looked at each other face-to-face.

"Why don't you want them edited?" Shada said, scared of her sister's response but needing to hear it nonetheless.

"You haven't even been edited yet and you've already let them do things I never would have thought you'd allow. Maybe it's better to keep them natural and let them live unburdened."

Shada couldn't help but feel attacked. The edits, and the procedure, were all so she could afford to pay back, then help, her sister. "Do you think I made the wrong decision?" Shada said, her head tilted to the side. Sparks of rage searched for fuel in her stomach.

"I think you've made a deal with the devil."

"Any deals I've made have been for us." The devil threw down tinder.

"I never asked you to do this."

"You didn't ask . . . You made me! Remember? You said I had to make money, and now that I am, now that I can help you get what you wanted, it isn't good enough." Small flames found kindling.

Sikya got up from the couch. "WestCorp is turning you into someone I don't even recognize anymore."

"WestCorp is helping me achieve my dreams! Why won't you let me help you do the same?" The fire burning inside Shada incinerated her exhaustion.

"Because my dream is to have a child and raise them in a world without WestCorp in it," Sikya said, her head bowed.

Shada stood up and her stomach rumbled, the fire ravenous for more fuel. She grabbed her backpack and headed for the door.

"Where are you going?" Sikya cried out.

Shada's plan was to get food, but the devil inside wanted her sister to worry. "Out," she said as she walked through the door, slamming it shut behind her.

CHAPTER THIRTEEN

"COME OVER TO MY PLACE," Chloe responded when Shada finished telling her over the phone about the fight she'd had with Sikya.

"Are you sure? I don't want to impose," Shada said. She hadn't heard Chloe talk about anyone in her life and sensed the woman valued her privacy.

"Positive! Stay here this weekend and we can go to the island on Monday."

Shada put forth a few more weak arguments to ensure she had done everything she could to provide Chloe a way out of the situation in case her friend was just being polite before she agreed, and Chloe gave her the address. "See you soon!" Shada said. According to her phone, the trip would take thirty minutes and require her to take a train to a neglected part of the city.

The closest train station to Chloe's home was on an elevated platform covered in graffiti. Shada could tell the different tags were words but couldn't make out what they said, their letters stylized beyond recognition. She didn't linger in case someone saw her and assumed she had an alliance with a rival. The turnstile at the bottom of the stationary escalator swung loose on its base. No employees were around to double-check if she had scanned her way through even though someone should have been, since the night was young and darkness had just descended. A cluster of tents were pitched below the platform, and dirty children ran around the bodies of passed-out parents beneath flickering streetlights.

Shada was catcalled multiple times on the walk from the station to Chloe's building. She was thankful for her size, knowing she could fight off an attacker if necessary. She gave the groups she passed a wide berth; they sat on the stairs of buildings and stood in the doorways of closed stores she wasn't sure would be open even in the brightness of day. Each time, their dull eyes paid her no attention as she passed, so she allowed herself to exhale but still listened for rapid footsteps behind her. She had a heightened state of awareness on her entire walk, a cycle of contract-relax every time she passed anyone or heard a voice call out to her.

Chloe's building had once required visitors to use the call box to enter, but Shada found a broken doorframe that kept the door open a few inches even when closed. She walked inside and up to her friend's apartment on the second floor. A green turf welcome mat sat in front. She knocked, saw the shadow of someone through the crack at the bottom of the door, then heard the door unlock and a chain slide off.

"Come in," Chloe said after she opened the door. She stepped back and allowed Shada to enter before closing the door and locking both locks.

Shada walked into a studio apartment full of plants. None of the plants had flowers, just green leaves of various size and shape. Shelves held smaller pots, and larger plants were arranged on the floor. The air inside made Shada realize the poor quality of the air she was used to breathing in the city. This air was crisp, cool, and a little damp, like the earth in which the plants grew. There was one bed, a couch, and, to Shada's surprise, no television.

"Make yourself at home," Chloe said.

"This is amazing," Shada said in awe while inspecting a shelf laden with pots. "How long did it take to collect all these?"

Chloe looked up at the ceiling, calculating. "A few years. The hardest part is finding them—there aren't exactly a bunch of plant stores in the city."

"I've never seen one, now that you mention it."

Chloe launched herself onto her bed and propped herself up on an elbow. "That hijack wore me out! I was asleep when you called."

Shada sat down on the couch and set her backpack on the floor next to her. "Sorry about that. I was exhausted when I got home too, but Sikya wouldn't let me rest." Shada again told Chloe how her sister disagreed with the way their money was made.

"She'll come around," Chloe said. With a twinkle in her eye she asked, "Would you do it again?"

"The hijack? Maybe, if someone wanted to pay."

"I was talking to the scientist who did my upload, and she said there are always people wanting to upload. There's a long wait list of people but not enough unedited who know about it."

Shada sat up, leaned forward, and set her elbows on her knees. "We're supposed to be edited this week."

"But what if we ask to get pushed back to the next group? We could get some cash, you for your loans and me for my farm. If we're going to work for the rest of our lives, what's the rush?"

Shada had a reason to rush: the sooner she got back into the league, the sooner her ban would begin. But, Shada thought, a major reason why she wanted into the league was to make enough money to pay off her debt and help her sister. She could do them both without having to wait until she was edited.

"It's not a bad idea. What do we have to do to make it happen?"

"The scientist told me to talk to Piper. I'd rather not, she rubs me the wrong way, but she's the facilitator."

"She does have a way of getting under the skin. Why wouldn't she mention it to us when we were first approached?"

"Maybe she figured we really want to be edited. The lady also said if someone is hijacked too many times, identity loss is possible. But I feel fine, and if we are losing ourselves when we get edited anyway, why not?"

Shada could tell Chloe's mind was already made up, that she'd be hijacked again. Shada still wasn't sure. Just then, a female voice came through a small speaker on Chloe's desk the size of a coaster. A series of numbers followed by a report of suspects getting away on foot towards dock number nine.

Chloe perked up and turned the dial on the small speaker. This time, a male voice could be heard. "Those assholes robbed a liquor store and are running to the abandoned warehouse!"

Chloe smiled and hopped off the bed. "Ready to have some fun?" she asked Shada. Without waiting for Shada's response, she said, "Let's go!"

Shada followed Chloe down the stairs and, once outside her building, away from the train station. The area got more civilized the farther they got from the station, with fewer homeless people and more light. Convenience stores were still open, and there was a bar within a few blocks that Chloe said she went to every so often.

Chloe turned right and ran towards the bay. Shada was surprised at how well Chloe maintained her pace as cop cars screamed by. They arrived at dock nine to find it blocked off by a semicircle of police cars. A series of warehouses stretched off into the distance.

"Can't go any farther, ladies," a cop said, holding up an outstretched hand.

Chloe backed up and beckoned for Shada to follow. Shada hadn't noticed Chloe grab the small speaker, but she pulled it—or another—from her pocket. The low volume required Chloe to hold the device up to her ear, and she told Shada what she heard.

"They followed two suspects and aren't sure which warehouse they're hiding in. Boats are at the far end of the dock, walling them in." Chloe was getting excited. "They are calling in the task force to search each warehouse." She put the speaker back into her pocket. "The search could take all night!"

"All night?" Shada groaned. "Didn't you say you were worn out too?"

"I was, but I can't miss this excitement! Some people go out on the weekends, I listen to the police scanners and try and see all the juiciest stuff in person. A few weeks ago there was a murder close to my house, and I was one of the first ones there!"

Chloe's excitement was infectious, and Shada got caught up in watching the spectacle unfold. Hours into the search, around four in the morning, multiple gunshots cracked out, and they witnessed one man get brought out on a stretcher and another in a body bag.

"That one guy is lucky, usually the task force doesn't let them live," Chloe said.

The next night, Saturday, after Chloe and Shada slept the day away and turned on the police scanner again, they found out that the robber who lived had shot his partner, turned himself in, and shot himself in the confusion.

CHAPTER FOURTEEN

SHADA CONVINCED Chloe to put the police scanner away early on Sunday night, and the two of them were able to get a full night's sleep before they went to the island Monday morning. The day's original plan was to receive their edits, but Chloe had already decided to speak to Piper about another hijack and assumed Shada would come with her.

Dozens of unedited humans were on the underground platform waiting to be taken to WestCorp. She could tell right away because on every one of her other trips, the platform was silent save for a few whispered conversations, none of which lasted long. In contrast, the platform on this day was filled with noisy and energetic unedited humans along with a mix of smells ranging from food to cologne. The normal commuters were present and recognizable by their stoicism, as if the unpleasantness was something to be tolerated once a month. The tram pulled up, ten cars long, and everyone filed inside and took a seat. Shada wondered why no screens descended from the ceiling. She decided it must have been because WestCorp knew why everyone was making today's trip, but they'd had no idea why she'd made her first trip.

The unedited all stared in awe at the massive security guards, who patted them down below the atrium before they were herded up the stairs by a WestCorp employee yelling from the top. He had on a short-sleeved white button-down, khaki pants, and black nonslip shoes.

"Everyone here for edits, this way please!" the young man said, gesturing behind him. With two orange wands in his hand he could have been an air traffic controller.

Shada and Chloe followed the crowd to the top of the stairs and saw a large part of the space in the atrium had been blocked off with velvet ropes. They waited for the last of the unedited passengers to pass before they asked to speak with Piper.

"She's very busy," the employee said without looking at them.

"It's about uploading consciousness into our bodies," Shada said.

The young man looked at the two of them, his eyes narrow with suspicion. "Are you from the papers?"

"No, we got the procedure last week. Can you just tell her we want to talk?" Chloe said.

The young man walked a short distance away, pulled a phone from his pocket, and talked to someone before returning to the two of them. "When I lead everyone away, just stay seated," he said.

Chloe and Shada took a seat behind the black velvet ropes with the rest of the unedited, and when everyone else was led away, they were left alone in a sea of tables and chairs. They stayed there for the next hour.

From what Shada could see, none of the edited humans paid them any attention. She was hungry and wondered if she had enough time to grab food when Piper appeared.

"Sorry, I had to give them the speech," Piper said.

"I thought you forgot about us!" Chloe said with a smile.

Shada could tell the expression on her friend's face was fake.

"Come to my office," Piper said.

They followed Piper through a series of corridors and ended up in a small office with two chairs, one on each side of a metal desk. There was no indication this was anyone's office, let alone someone who facilitated edits, and Shada thought she might have been assigned the space. Chloe took the seat across from Piper, and Shada leaned against the wall.

Piper got right to the point. "You were asking about another upload?" she said.

Chloe spoke first. "Are there other opportunities? I didn't mind the procedure."

"There are, but I must warn you: we have only uploaded multiple times in monkeys, never in humans."

"And what happened to the monkeys?" Shada asked.

"Up until the end, they were fine."

"The end?"

"Their last upload. Some were able to undergo the procedure over ten times, some over forty, before they lost the will to live."

The revelation was allowed to sink in before Chloe broke the silence. "But something like five times should be fine then, right?"

"It would be irresponsible of me to suggest a number, but more than five would never be allowed. Perhaps no more than three."

"How about you upload someone a couple more times and we see how we feel? The money was good, and if we're going to be edited in the end anyways, we want to make some money first," Chloe said, speaking for both herself and Shada.

"I'll make the arrangements. In the meantime, please feel free to stay on the island and make yourselves at home." Piper took Chloe and Shada to a waiting bus then led them to a dormitory. She made them each scan their thumbprint at the door and told them their finger would serve as their key. Chloe rushed into her room and hopped onto the bed. A loud thud rang out, followed by a groan. "There isn't a mattress," she said.

"I have a few questions," Shada said to Piper in the hallway while Chloe tensed in pain.

"I thought you might. You were quiet while your friend talked."

"I've been thinking a lot about employment after the edits. What's it like? Are you really happy all the time?"

Piper smiled. "It isn't so much happiness, it's just the absence of sadness." Her voice lowered. "I was unedited at birth and didn't receive edits until I was your age."

Shada was taken aback. She assumed Piper had been born edited; she didn't expect Piper to be similar to her. In the space of a blink, she wondered how many of the edited humans on the island had been born or made.

"The concept of working my entire life didn't seem satisfactory or desirable. But my parents used their house as collateral to pay for my education, and there was no way I would let them lose their home. Instead of suffering every day of my adult life, I decided to accept my fate. I had to agree to work here for years after, but with the money I make here, I am able to repay my debt and have paid off my parents' house, even though I feel no connection to them anymore."

"You didn't cut off the payments after you got edited?"

Chloe exclaimed how she could see the bay through her window.

"I made the necessary arrangements so the payments would continue to be withdrawn, regardless of the change in my DNA. I don't really have a choice."

Shada recalled Chloe's plan to buy her farm before the edits so her ultimate plan wouldn't change. She wondered about the process required to pay off Sikya's debt and provide for her future child and was grateful the edits wouldn't be undergone before the necessary arrangements were made.

"Most people work until they no longer have any usefulness to WestCorp. It's why there are so many people who want to be uploaded into an unedited body; they have nothing else to do while they wait to expire."

Shada nodded.

Chloe popped her head out of her room. "This is much nicer than my place, right, Shada?" she said.

"The view is, that's for sure," Shada replied.

Chloe walked into Shada's room and remarked how their rooms were mirror images of each other. "Your bathroom is on the left and mine's on the right," she said.

Piper asked if Shada was still on board with allowing an upload again.

Shada nodded, her plan of paying off both her and her sister's debt and providing a cushion for her sister to obtain a birth license before beginning her career solidifying in her mind.

"One more thing," Piper said as Chloe rejoined them in the hallway.

Shada's eyebrows raised higher as she waited for the woman to continue. Chloe looked confused, unaware of the conversation the other two were wrapping up. Piper pulled Shada into her room and shut the door on Chloe.

"Any future uploads you undergo will all be with Hollis. He doesn't like to share."

CHAPTER FIFTEEN

A KNOCK on the door woke Shada up. There were a few moments of frozen panic while she stared at the ceiling and tried to figure out where she was. She sat up, and the sterile room jogged her memory about her trip to the island the day before. Her phone had a notification for a missed call from Sikya. Shada snuck a finger into the thin ray of light that trickled in through the curtains and looked outside. The bay reflected the morning sun, and through squinted eyes she could make out small waves in the distance. The person outside knocked again, more impatient than before.

"Be right there," Shada called out.

She threw a T-shirt on and opened the door enough to look through the opening, bent sideways in order to hide her bare legs. Alfie smiled back at her and handed her a coffee.

"Time to get up," he said. "You're scheduled for upload in an hour."

"You guys don't waste any time," she said. Her jaw wasn't awake yet and words came out slurred. She accepted the black coffee and took a sip. It wasn't as strong as the kind she made herself, but the strength of this cup allowed for the smokiness of the roast to shine.

"Hollis enjoyed his experience last time and wanted to get going as soon as possible. I made him wait this long so you could get nine hours of sleep."

"Nine hours? I'm surprised I didn't jump out of bed," Shada said, shaking her head.

"It takes months to get used to the proper amount of sleep. Based on your vitals, I'd guess you sleep, what, six to seven hours a night?"

Shada thought about the two nights following the police scanner incident with Chloe. "If I'm lucky."

Alfie handed her a plastic card. "This will take care of your meals in the food court. Make sure you eat and are hydrated. Don't overdo it though, we don't want to have to find a bathroom on Hollis's time."

Shada nodded, wondering how she could be held responsible for the timing of her body's functions when she wouldn't even be in control of her body.

"Do you remember how to get to the reception hall?"

"The atrium?"

"Yes, can you get there on your own? All the transport vehicles going towards the center stop there. Even if you get on one going the wrong way, it will loop back around, you'll just have to wait."

"I can figure it out."

"Good, I'll see you there."

Remembering the activities Hollis had preferred on his last upload, Shada put on athletic clothes. She brushed her teeth right before she left. Chloe's door was still shut, and she wondered if her friend would be uploaded into that day as well. Maybe she'd already been woken up and was under someone's control right at that moment . . . If so, Shada didn't want to run into her, but she doubted WestCorp would let a chance encounter happen.

Shada got to the reception hall above the platform and decided to get another cup of coffee. The coffee wasn't the same quality as the cup Alfie had given her; this one was serviceable but nothing special. She got two hard-boiled eggs and a muffin for breakfast. Once she was finished, she surveyed the faces of the people crisscrossing the space while she listened to her body for signs of needing to go to the bathroom. She was in the middle of a roomful of people who all smiled at each other with their mouths but not their eyes, which made every one of them seem cold and detached.

She assumed the people who'd ridden the tram with her were all edited by now, and she was on the lookout for anyone she recognized from the day before. None of them seemed familiar. Maybe they needed time to adjust to their new DNA.

Shada spotted Alfie walking towards her from the direction of the lab. Instead of continuing towards her when their eyes met, he stopped short and waved her over. She drained the last of her coffee and threw her trash away on the walk over to him.

"Ready?" he said. This reminded her of a coach she'd had in high school who used to ask her the same thing before each game.

"As I'll ever be," Shada replied, the standard reply to her coach.

Alfie led her to the same room in which she had undergone the previous upload and instructed her to lie on the table. She sat down instead and watched Alfie turn on the equipment between the two tables. The monitor came to life, and Shada saw two pictures, one of Hollis and one of Piper, recognizable because of her dark red hair. Her physical metrics were listed beneath the photo.

"Piper?" Shada asked.

"She's been uploaded into before."

"By Hollis?"

"By Hollis. Please lie down," Alfie said.

"Isn't she edited? Why did Hollis want to upload into her?"

Alfie programmed the touch screen monitor while he talked. "You ask a lot of questions," he said with a chuckle. "Hollis was born edited and wanted to see what it felt like to upload into the body of a post-birth edited human before he took over an unedited. There was an upload into someone born edited before Piper too."

Shada lay down and folded her hands over her chest. "Why go through all the trouble?"

"We had to make sure his mind wouldn't crack. He's the head of WestCorp, remember?"

The weight of Hollis's position hit Shada, and she wondered why she had been the one chosen to host his mind, not once but twice. "And he was all right after uploading into my body?" she said. Shada felt ashamed of her unedited status and her associated emotions, which could have put the leader of WestCorp in danger of psychosis.

"Better than all right. He was rejuvenated! Right after he got out of your body, he tried to test how high he could jump and fell, almost broke his hip. There's a large bruise there now but it should be gone in a few days thanks to a new treatment still in development."

Shada apologized but didn't know why.

"Nothing to say sorry for, it wasn't your fault. If anything, it's mine. I'm the one who suggested he upload into your body. I thought he might want to feel what it was like to be an elite athlete. After we met, I suggested it to him when I went in to clear the plan we laid out to get you back into the league."

Shada felt a twinge of guilt for not getting into the league as soon as possible and allowing Hollis to upload again. It felt like she was playing with her future instead of playing the sport she loved.

The door opened while Alfie was adjusting the modified helmet on Shada's head, and Hollis walked in with a noticeable limp. "Good morning," he said, his mouth in the shape of a smile but his eyes unchanged.

"Morning, sir."

"Good morning," Shada muttered. She tried to nod, but the helmet kept her head in place.

Hollis lay on the table and put the helmet on his own head. "Shall we?"

Shada didn't have the chance to answer before her world went black.

CHAPTER SIXTEEN

SHADA THOUGHT she saw a faint circle of light far above, as if she was looking up from the bottom of a well. If she tried to focus on the light it would disappear, but by looking into the blackness ahead she could make out the outline of where the light existed. By switching her focus between the darkness and the spot where the light should be, Shada was able to bring the circle into focus. Once she could make out its edges, she concentrated on what was illuminated on the other side. The growing circle pushed the darkness away until it filled her entire field of vision. The brightness overwhelmed her, and she craved the darkness. It heard her desire and the edges of the circle of light constricted.

She reached for a breath in order to calm herself down. When she couldn't find the sensation, she instead counted to ten, some instinctual part of her knowing not to allow the darkness to return.

At the end of her count she saw the world through her own eyes, her body out of her control.

Alfie's arm poked in and out of her field of vision, relaxed as he walked. They were headed to a warehouse, walking through the sun past manicured gardens. Shada's head turned and watched Alfie's mouth move before her field of vision bobbed up and down. She knew her head had nodded in agreement to whatever Alfie said.

The doors ahead opened as they approached. Inside were rows of motionless humans laid out on stainless steel tables. Each human was attached to a blood transfusion machine, which Shada recognized from when her mother was on her deathbed.

Shada's head turned to look at Alfie's hand on her shoulder then looked at the head scientist's mouth. Shada heard herself say, "I'm sure," and a rush of noise flooded her awareness. The low hum of the climate control in the warehouse and the beeping of dozens, if not hundreds, of personal medical devices surrounded Shada's consciousness, and she felt the tug of silence reach out for her. By the time she counted to ten again, her body stood next to the bed of a woman in her early twenties wearing a hospital gown. Alfie grabbed the chart from the end of the woman's bed.

"The edited embryos didn't attach to her uterus," Shada heard Alfie say. Her own eyes stared at the woman's face. Shada realized the point of this exercise was to see if her body would react.

"Tension in the lower part of the throat, facial muscles contracting, urge to close my eyes," Shada heard herself report.

"General response," Alfie said. "Does it have any effect on your mind?"

Shada's field of vision shifted from left to right as she shook her head no.

"Good. Let's continue," Alfie said. They went through the back of the warehouse into a large refrigerator. One wall was filled with small square doors. Alfie opened one and rolled out a cadaver.

"This one died in childbirth," Alfie said. He paused. "Her children will grow up without a mother."

The dead woman became blurry.

"I know edited children don't have the same attachment to parental figures as the unedited do, so this won't matter to her offspring. But it does seem that this body has responded by filling both eyes with tears."

Shada watched a hand approach her face to wipe the tears away.

"And you are able to keep the response separate from your mind, correct?"

Hollis, in control of Shada, looked across the room with unfocused eyes. "No change in my internal state. Given time, I believe I could diminish, if not eliminate, these physiological responses." Shada's head whipped around to look at Alfie. "There's no way she's controlling the body without my knowledge, correct?"

"No, sir, your own consciousness has overridden hers. She's offline, for all intents and purposes."

"Good. I think we've seen enough. We haven't tested the response to torture and death, but I don't think it will be necessary."

"The pain portion is worth examining. It's a quick test."

Hollis-in-Shada sighed. "All right, if it's quick. I want to get some exercise again."

Shada tried to scream but nothing happened.

They went to the warehouse's security room, a room filled with camera monitors showing the rows of inanimate bodies, and Alfie borrowed a pistol from one of the massive security guards. He told Shada to back up.

"Ready?"

"As I'll ever be," Hollis-in-Shada said.

Alfie's head turned sideways, curious, then he shook away

whatever thought had occurred to him. He took aim and fired the electrical weapon.

When Shada regained her sight, she saw Alfie's face above her own, the stainless steel air ducts on the ceiling in the background. "Are you all right?"

Hollis nodded for Shada.

"Any adverse effects?"

"Stiff, sluggish limb control, localized pain in the impact site."

"And your mind? Do you still feel the same?"

"Still able to keep them separate."

Alfie smiled, and Shada got the sense his expression was a mirror of her own.

"This is good. I don't think we have anything to worry about. You should be able to maintain control of your consciousness regardless of circumstance."

"That's good to know. Let's not do that again." Her own hand reached down and pulled the electric darts from her stomach.

Shada agreed with Hollis, even though she never felt a thing.

The exercise Hollis wanted to perform turned out to be lifting weights. Alfie stood by as Hollis-in-Shada chose random machines and tested how heavy a weight the body he occupied could lift.

Shada watched herself in the mirror perform exercises she used to be forced to do with her team. She'd never cared about this aspect of being an athlete and therefore didn't bother to push the limits of what her body could do, so she was surprised when Hollis was able to urge her body to lift more weight than she ever thought possible. Since he could ignore Shada's body's signals about when to stop, he kept pushing past the point of exhaustion. Shada wondered if this weight-training session would affect her on the court but remembered she wouldn't have any meaningful time playing her sport for months to come, so it didn't matter.

It became clear over the course of the workout that Hollis used these machines on his own, because every time he lifted more weight inside Shada than he had in his own body, he remarked how frail his own body had become. He pushed weights around for almost an hour before Alfie coughed and told him it was time to get back to the room and switch back.

Hollis flexed Shada's biceps in the mirror and smiled, enjoying what he saw.

"We have to go," Alfie urged.

When the two of them walked back inside the room where the upload took place, Shada saw Hollis's body on the table taking small, even breaths. He could have been asleep. Without his force of personality he seemed frail, worn out, and cute, the way a grandfather might be. Alfie directed Hollis to lay Shada's body down on the table and placed the helmet on her head.

Shada woke up, back in control of her stiff and sore body, and wondered why she felt so alone even though Alfie and Hollis were in the room with her.

CHAPTER SEVENTEEN

When Hollis sat up on the metal table, his legs almost reached the floor. His back, bent with old age, forced his head forward, and when he spoke to Shada, who was sitting up on her own table, it appeared he was looking up at her from far below.

"Shada, I have to ask you something."

Alfie must have known what the old man had in mind, because he patted the old man's knee. "Sir, I'm not sure this is the right place or time."

Hollis glared at the scientist in response to the unwanted advice. "Damnit, Alfie, I'm running out of time and need an answer!"

Alfie hung his head and muttered, "You don't need an answer, you want an answer. There's already another workable solution."

"Don't waste my time getting hung up on the words I use," Hollis snapped. He turned his attention to Shada. "I'm dying," he said as a statement of fact.

"We all are," replied Shada. She wasn't in the mood to feel sorry for the man who'd agreed to have her electrocuted while in control of her body.

Hollis closed his eyes and tilted his head up. He took a deep breath and said, "I have cancer," with the exhale. "But it doesn't have to be the end." He looked at Shada with a thin-lipped smile pasted on his face.

"This is a bad idea," Alfie said, shaking his head.

"Quiet!" Hollis snapped.

Shada's eyes narrowed with suspicion. "What do you mean, it doesn't have to be the end?"

"It doesn't have to be the end if I could take over, permanently."

Shada looked down at her hands and picked at the cuticle on her thumb.

"I've tested negative experiences," Hollis blurted out. "I know we said the experiences would all be positive, but I had to check if I could maintain my identity under stress in an unedited body. It appears there won't be any problems, short of something catastrophic."

Shada launched into an internal debate about whether to tell the two men she'd been able to witness the tests. She decided to keep the information to herself. "What would have happened if your mind cracked while inside my body?"

"Well, once I got back inside my own body, I wouldn't have been able to have this conversation."

"We think," Alfie interjected. "This is a gray area; there haven't been many tests under these conditions."

Hollis nodded.

"Did you test negative experiences when you hijacked Piper?" Shada asked.

"Piper is edited, so she doesn't have the same emotional responses to misery as you do," Alfie said. "We did see how Hollis's mind responded to pain, and it seemed to be the same as if he was in his own body," Alfie said.

"Did you test the response to pain while in control of me?" Shada wanted them to admit it.

Hollis and Alfie both nodded.

"What did you do?" Shada knew the answer but wanted them to say it.

"Does it matter?" Alfie replied.

"Of course it matters! It's my body!"

"We administered an electric shock," Hollis said.

Shada closed her eyes for a moment before she looked right at Hollis. "Why not take over Piper? You already know it would work," she said.

"My original plan was to live in Piper, but she doesn't have the same physical capabilities as you. The upload into your body was going to be one last experience, for pleasure, before I transplanted my consciousness into her body."

"What about the security guards? They're massive."

"They're bred for size, not the strength of their neural connections. I have already accumulated a lifetime of knowledge. I need creativity. Another reason I prefer to upload into you instead of Piper."

"I'm not creative," Shada said. Between her and her sister, Sikya was the more creative one. She was better at writing and better at drawing. Shada had always been the athletic one.

"Being an athlete is creative. This lack of creativity is why edited athletes never do well in sports leagues. Alfie made me aware of this when he came to talk to me about getting you back into the league as a spokesperson for edited athletes."

"If you uploaded into my body, I wouldn't be able to be the spokesperson."

"That's correct."

Shada had heard all she cared to hear. "Why would I let you take my entire future from me?"

A wicked smirk appeared on Hollis's face. "Sikya."

Shada felt protectiveness rise from deep inside her. As a child she had always been the one to stand up to bullies, for Sikya and for her friends, and now that Hollis had spoken her sister's name, she felt like a child forced to stand up for her younger sister once again. "What about her?" Shada said, ready for a fight.

"She was rejected for a birth license." Hollis searched Shada's face to see how his first strike would affect her. "You knew that, right?"

Shada parried the blow. "She told me."

"She will continue to be rejected, unless you agree."

Shada felt the room slip away. The edges of darkness crept into her field of vision.

"Now, if you agree, Sikya will be approved within a few days of her next application. Guaranteed." Hollis had Shada backed into a corner and knew it.

The age of the two men in the room with her became apparent. Didn't they know an animal with no other options might attack? Shada sized them up and knew she could do a lot of damage, if not kill both of them before anyone could stop her. Hollis was worthless, so she would have to incapacitate Alfie first. Or maybe she could make quick work of Hollis before a more drawn-out fight with Alfie?

What stopped Shada from lashing out was the thought of Sikya never being able to have a child, the one thing her sister wanted in this useless world. She looked down at her palms and saw deep marks from where her fingernails had dug into her flesh.

Both Alfie and Hollis seemed amused as they watched Shada realize how hopeless her situation had become.

"You'll take care of her too? Provide enough money for her

to live with her child and still fight for the cause she believes in?"

"She'll find enough in her account to ensure she never has to worry about money again."

Shada considered the proposal. "All our debts would be paid?" She didn't want a loophole to ruin the plan; she'd seen enough genies grant three wishes to know to cover all her bases.

"Your debt, her debt, all gone. She'd be set for life."

Shada considered the proposal. She wanted to play in the league, yes, and considered the hijacks small setbacks to the initial plan she had formulated with Alfie. She also knew she couldn't face a future where her sister was denied a child.

If Sikya agreed to never have a child in order to keep Shada in control of her own body, Shada would feel guilty.

If Sikya never knew why each and every birth application was rejected, Shada would feel guilty.

Part of her wondered how much power Hollis, and by extension WestCorp, really had. Could they make sure the birth application was rejected? She didn't want to take the chance against such a powerful organization.

"Let me visit her one more time," Shada said.

"Are you agreeing to the transplant?"

Shada withdrew into herself before a thought struck her. "If I don't, could we still edit my blood oxygen levels so I can play in the league?"

Alfie looked at Hollis.

Hollis shook his head no. "Sorry. It's either this or nothing at all."

Shada wondered what she'd done in a past life to deserve this ultimatum. She sighed. "Then yes, I agree. I'll go visit her and come back."

"You'll only make it harder to follow through on your decision," Alfie said.

"If I don't go back, I won't do it at all," Shada retorted. "We got in a fight last time I saw her, and I'm not disappearing on her without seeing her again."

"Then go," Hollis said. "But you'd better hope I don't die before you get back."

CHAPTER EIGHTEEN

SHADA KNEW her future was slipping away. She made it back to the room WestCorp had provided and stopped outside her door, her thumb still on the scanner after she heard the door unlock, wondering where the last five minutes had gone. It was the same way she used to wake up from her daydream as the train pulled to a stop at her station after a grueling day of practice. She left her door open while she collected her belongings into her backpack.

Either Chloe had a sixth sense or Shada made more noise than she thought, because her friend appeared, leaning on the doorframe to Shada's room. Shada knew she was there but didn't want to engage. Chloe watched as Shada packed her bag.

"Where are you going?" Chloe said when Shada stood up to make sure she hadn't forgotten anything.

"Back into the city to see Sikya."

"What's going on?" Chloe said, her eyebrows raised.

Shada had trouble figuring out where to begin. She settled on: "Hollis wants to take over my body."

"Hollis?"

"The head of WestCorp."

"He wants to hijack you? What does it matter, you'll be asleep." A flash of recognition swept over Chloe's features and her eyes narrowed in suspicion. "Wait, how do you know who uploads? They won't let me know who takes over my body. I've asked."

Shada told Chloe how she had known it was Hollis from the first upload, and that he was now the one person allowed to upload into her body. She didn't mention how it didn't feel like she was asleep when her body was taken over. "He's dying," Shada said. She slung the backpack over her shoulder and exhaled. "And he wants to take over my body for good."

Chloe's mouth hung open. "What . . . what are you going to do? Will you let him?" she said when she regained control.

"He said if I don't, he'll make sure Sikya doesn't ever get approved for a child. I can't let that happen, it's all she's ever wanted."

Chloe told Shada to wait and that she was going back to the city with her. "They'll just have to wait until I get back to upload into me again!" she said as she walked out.

Left alone, Shada wasn't sure she wanted Chloe to come but didn't have the energy to put up a fight.

The two of them were silent as they made their way to and through the atrium, waited on the platform, and boarded the tram. Chloe broke the silence as they crossed over the bay. "So you're going to go through with it?" she said.

"I don't know!" Shada exclaimed, louder than intended. The handful of other passengers maintained their silence and acted like they didn't hear.

"You can't go through with it," Chloe said. She put a hand on Shada's thigh. "I have to tell you something."

"What?"

"It's something I've done since the first upload. I didn't trust them, I thought they might want to take over our bodies from the start, so I took . . . precautions."

Shada's suspicious eyes searched Chloe's face for clues. "We both did, at the office."

"No, separate from that." Chloe took a deep breath and took her time exhaling. "I've poisoned myself before each time. When I get back into my body, I take the antidote." Chloe pulled a pair of small vials from a pocket in her backpack, one red and one blue. "The guards never found them," she said. "I think they only look for weapons, maybe recording equipment."

"What if they wanted to upload more than once?"

"The poison has an eight-hour dormant period before it takes effect. As long as I take the antidote within that window, I'm fine."

Shada reached for the vial of red liquid, but Chloe withdrew her hand. "How did you find out about this?" Shada asked.

Chloe put the vials back into her backpack. "My mother was a botanist. She developed organic compounds that could be used as weapons for the military. When she found out the plan was to use them in the event of an unedited uprising, she threatened to go public and was discharged. Then blacklisted by every major company. Those are from her stockpile."

Shada hung her head. "They aren't giving me a choice. If I don't agree, they won't even perform the edits to get me back in the league."

Chloe's confused look prompted Shada to tell her about the plan she and Alfie had come up with for her to be the face of edited athletes.

"So we wouldn't have been working together until your playing career ended . . ." Chloe said, her voice trailing off. "Why didn't you tell me?"

"You didn't tell me about the poison."

They stared at each other, each daring the other to blink, as the train came to a stop beneath the city. "What's done is done," Shada said.

"Agreed."

They disembarked, left WestCorp's pristine platform beneath them, and stopped at the bottom of an escalator that was part of the city's transportation system.

"I need to talk with Unedited Rights and set it up so everything goes to Sikya once I'm taken over," Shada said.

Chloe nodded to the platform on the level on which they stood. "I'm going to run home and grab more vials. I didn't plan for them to let us live on the island."

"Meet me at my place when you're done." Shada took Chloe's phone and put in her address. "I should be there in a few hours."

Shada took the train to the Office of Unedited Rights. Tensen wasn't there, but she was able to talk to another advocate. Without explaining that she would be taken over, not edited, she filled out the necessary paperwork to transfer all future funds to Sikya. While signing the paperwork, she wondered what would happen to Hollis's assets, if they would somehow get transferred to her as well since he'd be dead. If so, would Sikya be entitled to all of it?

The process took twenty minutes, and before Shada knew it she was on the train to her apartment. As she approached her building, she tried to figure out the best way to break the news to her sister. She rode the elevator up, still not sure of the best way to start. Just outside their door, she determined she would make amends before bringing up her own next steps.

Shada walked into an empty apartment. Sikya wasn't home, and there was no sign of when she would be back. Shada sat on the couch to wait and didn't put up a fight when sleep overtook her.

A knock woke her. She wiped drool from her mouth and

flexed her hand to regain feeling before she stood up to answer the door.

Chloe beamed a smile at her before Shada's lack of reciprocation wiped it from her face.

"She's not here," Shada said.

"Did you want to wait for her?" Chloe asked.

Shada thought for a moment before she shook her head no.

"Leave her a note," Chloe suggested.

Shada grabbed a pencil and the pad of paper they used for their grocery list. She hunched over the counter and couldn't think of the right words to say.

Thinking out loud, Shada said, "If I tell her I'm getting the transplant so she can have a kid, she'll get mad at me." She tapped the eraser on the counter. "And if I say I'm getting edited but won't be playing in the league so don't expect to hear from me again, she'll feel abandoned because I could make money playing overseas without leaving her behind."

Shada looked at Chloe and her friend shrugged.

In the end, Shada wrote one word: sorry.

CHAPTER NINETEEN

SHADA GRABBED an apple from the pile on the counter, because Sikya would have wanted her to take one, and grabbed the rest of the red gummy bears from the cabinet. Together she and Chloe walked back to the train station, Shada for the last time. She was about to give her apple to the homeless man and his dog when she saw a pile of pristine red apples behind them, stacked against the chain-link fence. Sure they were the ones she had donated to them on her previous trips, and wondering how they were able to last so long, she kept the apple for herself to see how long it would take to rot. They rode the tram back to the island and were informed that preparations for both their procedures had begun.

Chloe was hijacked into twice in the days Shada waited. Shada assumed, but never asked, that Chloe took the poison before she left each time.

A cleaning lady made sure Shada didn't need anything before she went into Chloe's room during the second hijack. Shada feared it might be a ploy to search Chloe's belongings, and she hoped they didn't find and take her vials of antidote.

Later that evening, Shada heard a thump through their shared wall as Chloe collapsed onto her metal bed.

Piper showed up outside Shada's room while Shada lay awake in the brightness of morning, staring at the ceiling and listening for movement in the adjacent room so she could be sure Chloe was still alive. "Shada, it's time," she said after a crisp knock on the door.

Shada got dressed and gathered the rest of her belongings, not knowing what to do with them since she'd have no use for them once the hijack was done. She made Piper wait in the hall as she banged on Chloe's door to wake her up.

"What?" Chloe groaned.

"I want to say goodbye," Shada said.

Chloe opened the door an instant later. Her eyes were puffy, and indented lines crisscrossed her face from the fabric of the pillow. Chloe looked like she wanted to say something but instead threw her arms around Shada.

Shada imagined the hug was transmitted through Chloe to Sikya via some unknown means of transfer.

Piper coughed and the friends separated. They lingered for a moment, each waiting for the other to say something, but when neither of them said a word they exchanged a nod. Shada turned away and followed Piper down the corridor.

"Another upload?" Piper said.

Shada thought it was a weird attempt at making conversation. "Today's the day," she replied.

"Did you know this was my idea?"

"Alfie said it was his idea for Hollis to upload into my body."

"That was his idea. Uploading consciousness in the first place was my idea."

"Really? I thought Alfie developed it."

"He did develop it, after I asked him if it would be possible. For the idea, I was promoted to Hollis's lieutenant."

They walked outside into the blazing sun. A two-person transport pulled up to them and its door flung open. Shada climbed on board and sat next to Piper with her backpack on her lap, watching the manicured lawns pass by.

Piper interrupted Shada's appreciation of the last moments in control of her own body. "Hollis has uploaded into me too, you know, and he'll be back. You're just the flavor of the week."

Shada realized Piper had no idea the switch was about to be permanent.

"We have a good thing going, so don't think you'll get edited and take over as his second-in-command. I've come too far to let you take this away from me."

"I don't want to work for him."

Piper ran out of ammunition without Shada's engagement. They walked through the atrium and took another small transport vehicle to the side of the island farthest from the city across the water. They got off outside a short cement building with a thick metal front door and no windows. Its roof slanted down towards the edge of the water. There were a few palm trees scattered about, but nothing outside suggested the purpose of the building.

Shada had dismissed Piper's threatening attitude until then, but in this remote corner, she wondered if she meant to harm her.

"This is Hollis's personal residence," Piper said. She grabbed Shada's shoulder and spun her so the two of them were face-to-face. Her index finger hovered in front of Shada's nose. "Don't forget, I won't let you ruin this for me."

Piper let go and walked to the front door. She opened up a hidden control panel and placed her face in front of a scanner. The large metal door groaned to life as multiple locks disengaged. Piper pushed the door open and led Shada inside.

Lights blinked on, and Shada saw a room in sharp contrast

with the exterior. The walls were made of wood and looked like they had been taken from an old wooden ship. There were two sofas, both dark brown leather, and on the walls multiple large fish were mounted in a bent position. The floor was covered with a dense purple area rug. On the wall opposite the front door was a stainless steel elevator door.

"Sit," Piper commanded.

Shada sat on the edge of one couch with her backpack behind her, and Piper sat across from her.

"Alfie should be here to get you soon," Piper said. She stared at Shada with a murderous glint in her eye.

"How many times were you hijacked?" Shada asked, to kill the silence between them. She was pleased to see Piper flinch at her word choice.

"I was uploaded into three times."

"You said yourself multiple hijacks could have an adverse effect. Are you sure it didn't cause you to go crazy?"

If the intensity of Piper's glare could be measured it would be off the charts.

Shada realized that, even though they were the same height, the woman across from her was frail. She laughed as her fear of physical harm dissipated.

"What's so funny?" Piper said.

"Nothing," Shada said.

Faint beeps from the rising elevator got louder as it approached the level where the two women sat. They both stared at the door as it opened and Alfie strode out.

"Shada, good to see you again," the scientist said with a smile. Shada closed her eyes, the weight of her decision getting heavier by the moment.

"Piper," he said with a nod.

Hollis's lieutenant popped up and smiled. She seemed eager and approachable.

"This way," Alfie said to Shada with a gesture towards the elevator.

Piper walked forward before Alfie held up a hand to stop her. "Thanks for bringing her here. You are no longer needed."

Piper looked like she'd been hit in the stomach so hard the air was driven from her lungs. She stammered something about being second-in-command and how Shada was unedited. The disdain in her voice was palpable.

"We need Shada, not you."

Piper didn't move.

"We'll call you if we need anything." Alfie waited for Shada to get onto the elevator before he joined her inside. He pushed the number at the bottom of a column of buttons, a seven, and the elevator doors shut, leaving an angry Piper behind.

"She's upset because Hollis doesn't let her down here," Alfie said, shaking his head.

Shada nodded, surprised at how something could matter so much to someone who had been edited. She thought toxic ambition should be addressed in the standard edits too.

CHAPTER TWENTY

THE ELEVATOR DOORS OPENED, and Alfie led Shada into a large underground cavern. The ceiling above was smooth stone with a grid of light bulbs hanging from wires. Shada stared down a long corridor with white walls that ended at a standard height, well below the level of the stone above. At the end was an open space occupied by a dark brown dinner table, its ends obscured by the walls.

"This way," Alfie said, striding forward with purpose.

Shada followed the scientist past multiple doorways without doors. One room had ancient scientific equipment, analog dials, and beige plastic coverings, all coated with dust. Another room had a television and a couch with a blanket thrown in a pile on one armrest. The third room Shada was led past held exercise equipment, and the fourth held a computer on a desk surrounded by piles of books. If left to her own devices, she would have gone into the study and seen what kind of books the leader of WestCorp kept in his residence.

The table at the end of the corridor was massive, the largest table Shada had ever seen. She took a quick count of the chairs: twenty. Nine on each side and one on each end. She wondered what kind of dinners Hollis had hosted, because she'd never gotten the impression he was one for large social gatherings. A vision came to her of Hollis at one head of the table surrounded by powerful figures from both the city and industry.

On the left of the table was an industrial kitchen full of stainless steel appliances and large open spaces for a chef to work. Two doors on the right side of the room, the only doors she had seen so far, were closed.

"Please take a seat," Alfie told her.

Shada sat down in the middle of the table with her back to the elevator. She set her backpack on the floor next to her, withdrew her red gummy bears, and began popping them into her mouth one at a time. She was intent on finishing the bag before the chance was taken from her by Hollis. In front of her was a bare wall of shiny black rock. The rock wasn't smooth, and its edges reflected the light, giving Shada the impression thousands of small eyes were all looking at her.

Alfie walked over to the two doors and knocked on the one on the left. From the door on the right came the reply. "I'm in here," Hollis called out.

Shada thought his voice sounded weaker than she remembered, but within its feebleness lay a definitive quality she found interesting.

Alfie opened the other door, and Shada saw Hollis lying down on one of two stainless steel tables in a small room. Compared to the other rooms, this one could have been a closet. It was just large enough to accommodate the two tables.

Hollis got up from the table and walked into the room with the large table.

"How do you feel, sir?" Alfie asked.

"Like I'm a hundred. Every bone hurts."

"You won't have to feel that way much longer," Alfie said. His face was unchanged, but the smirk shone through.

Hollis walked toward the kitchen. As he passed Shada, he reached down and squeezed her shoulder. At the same time he replied to Alfie, "I know."

Shada watched as Hollis opened the refrigerator and pulled out a plate covered with aluminum foil.

"One last meal?" she asked. The wavering of her voice embarrassed her, and the faint echo she imagined wouldn't let her brush it off.

"My favorite," Hollis said with a timid smile. "Roast beef, mashed potatoes, and green beans. My mother used to make it for me when I was young."

Even powerful men are sentimental when faced with their own mortality.

After Hollis grabbed a fork and knife, he sat down at the end of the table closest to the kitchen. Shada got the sense he had spent many of his meals sitting at that very spot with nothing but empty chairs for company. Alfie sat next to him.

"You're going to eat it cold?" Shada asked.

"Doesn't matter to me, it still tastes the same," Hollis replied.

Shada and Alfie watched Hollis eat his last meal, having never been offered anything to eat themselves. He was a slow eater, relishing each bite because they were his last. Twice he leaned back in his chair—each time Shada was certain he was done—but both times Hollis leaned forward to resume until the food was gone.

When Hollis leaned forward and rested his elbows on the table with an empty plate in front of him, Alfie asked him if he was ready.

"Let's get this over with."

Hollis didn't bother to clear his used dishes, he just stood up and began walking into the small room. Alfie gave Shada a nod towards the same room and she followed him inside.

"Onto the table, you two," Alfie said. His voice was jovial, an attempt to lighten the mood in what was about to be the end of both Shada's and Hollis's existences as they knew it.

"Will this switch be stronger?" Shada asked Alfie as she climbed onto the stainless steel table.

"Nope, it'll be the same feeling as before."

"And it will be permanent?"

"It will be, because there won't be a switch back. In theory, all of the other uploads could have been permanent too, that's why you had to visit the guys over at Unedited Rights so they could make sure we put everyone back into the body where they belong."

Hollis was the picture of serenity on his table. His head rested on the pillow, his eyes were closed, and his hands were folded on his chest.

Alfie pushed on Shada's shoulder to get her to lie down. Once he deemed her position satisfactory, he placed the helmet on her head.

"What's going to happen to his body? Are you going to keep it alive?"

"He has orders to kill this vessel after the switch," Hollis said. His voice was distant and could have come from the far side of the massive table.

Alfie moved over to Hollis's side and placed the helmet over his head with a delicate touch. The moment they both had their helmets on, Shada felt a surge of energy that had nothing to do with the machine between them. It was as if the whole situation became real in an instant. Her stomach leapt, her heart raced, and her skin crawled, knowing she would be taken over at the flip of a switch.

She closed her eyes and counted out ten shallow breaths while Alfie adjusted the machine between the two tables. She imagined the last time she saw Sikya and hoped the note she left wouldn't cause her sister more pain.

"Ready?" Alfie said.

Shada turned her head and looked past Alfie as Hollis nodded yes. Her eyes met Alfie's and she nodded yes too.

Alfie counted down. "Three . . . two . . ."

At the last moment, at the same moment Alfie said "One," Shada thought of her backpack on the ground next to the table and wondered what would become of her belongings.

CHAPTER TWENTY-ONE

IT HAD TAKEN time for Shada to see the world through her own eyes during the previous uploads, so she was surprised when she was able to witness her surroundings while Hollis, in control of her body, still lay on the table. Through a series of rapid blinks, she saw the ceiling come into focus as the dark circle receded. Her head turned, and she saw Alfie shift his gaze between Hollis's old body and the monitor as if expecting the delivery of an important package. Then, Shada's eyes closed, plunging their previous master into darkness.

"I feel dizzy," she heard herself say. Her voice was pitiful and weak, a voice she used when she was sick and she wanted Sikya to do something for her. Hollis, in charge of her body and therefore in charge of the tone of her voice, had no way of knowing this. He must have taken on this particular inflection in his old age, and it remained after the body his mind occupied had lost decades.

"You've felt dizzy every other time too. This will pass," Alfie said.

Hollis opened Shada's eyes and watched a spike on the monitor between the tables hold Alfie's attention.

"This is the last chance," Alfie said, his face serious. "Are you sure?"

"Let it go," Hollis said from Shada's body.

Inside, Shada could only imagine herself screaming.

A few minutes later, Alfie announced Hollis's body was dead. "No going back now."

"Never intended to. Time to make myself at home." Hollis-in-Shada stood up and looked down at his corpse.

Shada wondered what the sensation felt like and hoped it was more jarring than her own experience of being hijacked.

"Get rid of it," he said with a wave of her hand.

"Do you care how?" Alfie asked.

"How do we get rid of the bodies of the stray dogs? Burn 'em? Do that."

"Will do, sir," Alfie said without so much as an extra blink.

Hollis-in-Shada walked through his bedroom to the attached bathroom. Shada hoped he would turn her head to look at the rest of the bedroom, but he kept her eyes forward, focused on his destination. He stared at her face in the mirror, and Alfie appeared in the open doorway.

"Who else should be allowed to know about the switch?" Alfie asked.

Shada's gaze jerked from the mirror to Alfie. "Nobody! Not a single person. Tell everyone I'm bedridden, too sick to leave my residence."

"So I'll have to burn your body myself," Alfie said, his voice trailing off. "I'll do it tonight."

"Whatever you have to do," Hollis-in-Shada said. He returned his gaze to the mirror and leaned forward, pulling the bottoms of his eye sockets down to inspect Shada's pupils. Shada watched as her eyes crossed then looked far left, then far right. Her mouth opened and Hollis inspected her teeth. "She took care of herself," Hollis-in-Shada muttered.

"Agreed. You made a good choice."

Shada couldn't help but feel a perverse sense of pride at their approval.

"What are you going to do about clothes?" Alfie asked.

"I hadn't thought about it. Let's see what she has in her bag."

Shada's body was taken into the large room, and she watched as Hollis bent down and grabbed her bag. Upon inspection, Hollis found one more pair of shorts and two more T-shirts, each of which had already been worn multiple times in the previous week. He pulled out the apple Shada had taken from home, stared at it for a moment, then tossed it back into the bag.

"We've got to get you more clothes," Alfie said.

"Go topside and grab them," Hollis-in-Shada commanded. He set her bag onto a chair and slid the chair back under the table. "But make sure it's the kind of clothes she'd wear. I don't want anyone to think anything has changed."

"I can do that," Alfie said. He stood still next to Shada's body, his hands resting on the back of a chair.

"Now," Hollis said.

Alfie told Hollis he was planning to do it when he took Hollis's dead body later that night, then he turned and walked to the elevator. The sound of his footsteps fading into the distance echoed off the walls of the cavern. Hollis watched through Shada's eyes as Alfie got into the elevator.

Alone, Hollis-in-Shada went back into the bathroom. Shada watched as Hollis took her shirt and sports bra off to inspect her bare chest, then pulled her waistband away from her body and looked at her tuft of pubic hair. Shada thought she should feel more scandalized, but without any sensations from her body, the inspection seemed scientific. Without words she wasn't able to sense whether Hollis was aroused, and without this feedback there was no sense of shame.

Hollis released the shorts and pulled the shirt back down. He walked into the room with exercise equipment and Shada saw the depth of this room, unknown to her when she'd walked past the first time. There was enough space for every machine he had used the last time he exercised her body, and he got to work pushing himself on the same exercises in the same order.

Towards the end of the routine Shada could hear her body's ragged breaths. Shada expected Hollis to end the routine with another flexing of her muscles, but instead he jumped on a treadmill. Over the next twenty minutes he increased the pace past the point of what she thought possible. In the mirror she could see her own chest heaving and the strain of sustaining the speed on her face. Her own mind couldn't sense the effort her body was exerting, but she tried to count to ten breaths, her standard method of calming herself down when she got too spun up during exercise.

Watching her face to determine the correct timing, Shada counted ten breaths before she began a second count. By the time she reached four, she could sense, in the same fashion she had been able to see the faint circle from the bottom of the well, the presence of her diaphragm. She tried to latch on to the feeling but lost it before she could reach the count of one.

She began another countdown and was able to find her breath without reliance on sight. From ten through seven it tickled the edge of her awareness, from six to three she could identify it, and from two to one she let it take over the entirety of her awareness. It was easy to let it take over since her mind was starved for physical connection, like finding an oasis in the middle of a desert. She exerted control over her breathing, forcing her stomach out with every inhale. She stared at the mirror, looking for signs in her face of whether or not Hollis was aware of her presence. The muscles in her face relaxed as her breath become more controlled, but there was no indication Hollis knew why.

Shada held on to the control of her breathing through the final three minutes of her body's time on the treadmill. The sensation served as a beacon of hope, a tether she could latch on to in the nothingness of space.

Hollis stopped the workout and dismounted. Shada was covered in sweat.

As Shada's heart rate fell and her breathing became more regular, she felt control of her breath slip away. It was a slow descent into the vacuum, but after spending time grounded, it felt like she lost control of her body all over again.

As Hollis-in-Shada took a shower, Shada couldn't help but feel a glimmer of hope. If she could learn to control her body's breathing under normal circumstances, could she one day hope to take over her limbs as well? Then she'd be able to take over her body altogether while still having access to Hollis's resources.

And Hollis would be the one trapped inside.

CHAPTER TWENTY-TWO

HOLLIS HAD PLOPPED Shada's body on the couch and was watching a financial news report when the elevator's gears sprang into action. Hollis didn't bother to move, and he showed no other signs of preparing for a guest, so Shada assumed it was Alfie coming back. She figured the scientist must be one of the few people with access to the space. Now Shada, since Hollis occupied her body, was part of this exclusive list.

A beep rang out as the elevator door opened and footsteps approached.

"In here," Hollis-in-Shada yelled.

Alfie's head appeared around the corner. It seemed as if he wanted to withhold the full arrival of his body until he was sure Hollis was ready to receive him. Shada wasn't sure if this style of entrance was a normal occurrence or if he'd added in the momentary pause because Hollis now resided in a woman's body.

"What are you waiting for?" Hollis said. He sat up on the couch and adjusted the blanket draped over Shada's long legs.

Alfie walked in with a beige fabric bag in each hand. He set them down on the coffee table and withdrew what he brought.

"I brought our standard athletic shorts and T-shirt," he said, pulling these items from the first bag and holding them up.

Hollis-in-Shada nodded.

"And these are some of our other standard outfits." He showed off a dark blue jumpsuit. "This is what the mechanics and gardeners wear."

Shada couldn't sense her face's response, but Alfie responded by stuffing the jumpsuit into the bottom of the bag.

"And this is what we give our people who work in the service sectors." Alfie showed off a pair of khaki pants and a short-sleeved white polo shirt.

Hollis held out one of Shada's hands and accepted the shirt from Alfie. "This could work." He picked up the pants and pulled on the fabric, remarking on their stretchiness. "Give me two more of this outfit, and three more of the athletic gear." He threw the pants and white shirt onto the coffee table and leaned back on the sofa.

"I'll get right on it. How are you feeling?"

"Tired, to tell you the truth." Hollis looked at the clock: 6:00 P.M. "It's still early, but I think I'll get ready for bed soon."

"I'm not surprised, these uploads tend to be exhausting for the host." Alfie stuffed the clothes in the bag and told Hollis he would put the approved clothes into his room and take the other ones topside.

"Did you need anything else?" Alfie asked.

"Yes, as a matter of fact. Two things. One, find a diet for athletes. This body's going to need more fuel than what I used to consume, and I'm not sure where to start. I want to keep her in peak condition."

"You mean 'myself'; this is your body now. I'll get a dietitian right away. Did you want to meet with them or just have the meals made for you and brought down according to their recommendations?"

"Just have the meals brought down," Hollis said. Shada wondered if someone other than Alfie would be coming into the underground residence in order to deliver the food.

"What's the second thing?"

"Bring two women down tomorrow night," Hollis-in-Shada said.

Alfie's lack of surprise at the request suggested to Shada it had been made before.

Alfie glanced at Shada's crotch before he looked up and said, "Will you be participating as well, or do you just want to watch?"

"Just watch," Hollis-in-Shada said.

"Any preferences?" Alfie said.

Hollis paused then told Alfie to make sure they were good-looking.

Shada was disgusted at the nonchalant way these arrangements were made.

Alfie left the room and moments later walked past on his way back to the elevator.

Hollis waited for the beeps to stop before he got up and walked Shada's body to his bedroom. There was a large bed with one dark gray pillow and a matching comforter, a dresser, and a cushioned chair made of dark brown leather that matched the couch in front of the television. On the chair was the bag Alfie had left with the two outfits Hollis had decided to keep, more of the same on the way.

Shada was surprised Hollis's bedroom wasn't larger until she remembered this entire underground chamber was his, and now in a weird way, hers.

Hollis tossed the bag of clothes into his closet—Shada would have winced if she had control of her face, because she detested clothes on the floor—and climbed into bed without taking off any clothes.

Shada heard the elevator descend in the middle of the night. Padded footsteps then walked the length of the corridor and into the kitchen. She assumed it was the meal delivery, so she wasn't curious when the refrigerator opened, closed a bit later, and the footsteps walked back to the elevator.

Her body stayed asleep the whole time. True sleep paralysis. She hated the sensation.

Hollis must have expected the overnight delivery, because the first thing he did in the morning was check the refrigerator. Meals were labeled one, two, three, and four, and each had a suggested time range written on the label. There were three days' worth of food, including that day. When Hollis inspected the day's food, Shada saw meals one, two, and four corresponded to breakfast, lunch, and dinner, and meal three was a lighter snack.

Hollis spent the day the same way he had spent the previous. There was exercise followed by time on the couch watching television. Since he didn't do any work, Shada wondered if this was a planned vacation from WestCorp, intended to give him time to adjust to life inside a new body. It didn't occur to her that this was the weekend and she had glimpsed Hollis's life on Saturday and Sunday.

Alfie showed up during dinner flanked by two women in skintight cocktail dresses. Both showed off long legs. One was blond, with pale skin and high cheekbones. The other looked to be foreign, with olive skin that couldn't be placed and smoky eyes. Both were beautiful, and any man would agree they were of equal quality, just different flavors.

"These are for you," Alfie told Hollis-in-Shada.

Hollis invited the two women to sit down while he finished his meal and told Alfie he would send the women up in two hours, a statement that Alfie interpreted as a dismissal. The two women seemed both confused and impressed that a brown-skinned woman such as Shada had so much power and lived in an underground bunker.

They tried to make conversation by asking how the food was, but Hollis ignored them both while his last bites disappeared. When his meal was finished, he told both women to climb onto the table.

They looked at each other for a moment, a hesitation that caused Hollis to say, "Now!" in Shada's voice.

The women climbed onto the table and kneeled, awaiting further instruction. Hollis told them to make out with each other. He leaned Shada's body back in her chair to enjoy the show.

Within minutes both women were down to their bra and panties, as commanded by Hollis-in-Shada.

Shada saw the way they watched her face, looking for signs of approval. When none came, the blond woman wrapped her arm around the one with smoky eyes to remove her bra.

"Stop," Hollis said. He muttered under his breath. "This body is useless."

"What's wrong?" the blond woman asked.

"It's not working," Shada heard herself say.

"You could join us," the other woman suggested, her smoky eyes glinting with mischief.

"This body has no response whatsoever."

If Hollis could communicate with Shada, she'd be able to tell him she'd never been attracted to women.

"Put your clothes back on and get out," a dejected Hollis told the women. The voice sounded more like Shada's own tone than anything else he had said since the hijack. "You can wait on the couches outside the elevator. Someone will pick you up at the end of your two hours."

After watching the two escorts grab their dresses and shuffle to the elevator, Hollis-in-Shada walked into his bedroom and shut the door. He laid on the bed for a moment before going into the bathroom and looking into the mirror. For the first time, Shada saw herself look frustrated and felt proud of her body for ruining Hollis's evening.

CHAPTER TWENTY-THREE

Hollis-in-Shada emerged from his underground residence on Monday morning and went straight to his office attached to the atrium. It was a massive space that held a solitary wooden desk and two chairs, giving visitors the impression they had a long way to walk from the door to their seat across from him. He had two secretaries: an older man in charge of his schedule and a younger woman who took care of paperwork. They both stared at Hollis, who now occupied Shada's body, as he walked in like he owned the place.

"Good morning," the young woman said. "Can I help you?" She had short brown hair in curls and too much makeup.

From her reaction, Shada could tell Hollis shot her a look of reproach. The older male secretary interjected to diffuse the situation.

"Good morning, Shada," he said. He had dark skin, an African accent, and could have been anywhere from thirty to fifty. "Alfie mentioned you would be joining us from now on." He looked at the younger secretary and his eyes widened.

Hollis looked down at Shada's hand as if reminding himself of his changed outward appearance.

"That's right."

"My name is Ernie, and this is Beth." Hollis-in-Shada introduced himself as Shada and shook both their hands.

"Hollis also said not to walk in on you when you are in the office. If we need you, we can call." The older secretary was reminding his counterpart about the rules that had been established.

Shada saw her world shift up and down as Hollis nodded. Hollis walked into the office, shut the door, and the moment he sat down at his desk he called Alfie.

"I need you to do an assessment," Hollis said.

Alfie paused before he replied. It was obvious he wasn't used to hearing Shada's voice tell him what to do, and the new interaction took a moment to register. "I can do one right after lunch, I'll call when I'm ready. It should be around two," he said. Even though Shada had had limited interactions with the scientist, she could tell he was exasperated after dealing with Hollis the entire weekend, but she wasn't sure Hollis could tell or, if he could, cared.

"After lunch then," Hollis said before ending the call.

Hollis spent the morning doing computer work. Shada had never been good at sitting still, and it seemed Hollis was now learning what it was like to be unedited while trying to do work in an environment optimized for edited humans. The incongruence caused Hollis-in-Shada to walk around in frustration multiple times per hour. Lunch, brought from his residence, was eaten at noon, in accordance with the label. Lunchtime was spent dealing with a lawsuit courtesy of the Office of Unedited Rights.

At one thirty Hollis lamented how time never cooperated, slowing down and speeding up in direct contradiction to what was necessary. Shada heard his complaints and wondered if he'd said them to himself or for her.

Two came and went without a call from Alfie. It wasn't until almost three that Alfie called Hollis's office and told him to come to the lab.

"Sorry, I was busy putting out fires," Alfie explained.

"On my way," Hollis said before rushing out, without acknowledging Alfie's explanation.

Shada's long strides ate up the distance to the transport vehicle that took Hollis to the lab, and soon her body was seated on an examination table. Alfie's disheveled hair and stained lab coat inspired a host of questions in Shada, but Hollis ignored the scientist's physical state.

"What's going on?" Alfie said.

Hollis looked around the room before he began. "Is it possible for this body's previous owner to influence any of my actions?"

Shada could feel another awareness searching for sensation as soon as these words left what used to be her mouth. It was as if by identifying a channel of connection, and looking for its existence, Hollis had created it himself. Shada felt her breath and dove into its steady rhythm, a grounding presence she had missed during her time in isolation.

"What makes you say that?" Alfie asked as he sat down on a wheeled stool.

"Last night, with the girls, I felt nothing."

"Your biological responses won't be the same as before. Shada brought her own likes and dislikes to the table, and you'll have to learn what they are."

"But I still like the same things!"

"You need to reframe your mindset. You are now inside this body. For example: if you liked pickles, and Shada hated pickles, you won't like pickles anymore."

Shada took full control of her breathing while Hollis explored the repercussions of consciousness transplantation with Alfie. She held an inhale for the briefest of moments, to see if it could be done, but released the breath before Hollis picked up on the change.

"But I still think the same!" Hollis-in-Shada said.

"That's the thing! You don't. You're still clinging to old thought patterns and aren't making space for the full spectrum of what you can now accomplish. There's a reason you didn't switch into a member of security; you wanted her creativity. Have you been inspired at all?"

"All I've noticed is that I can't pay attention the same way I used to."

"Because you aren't in an edited body anymore. Embrace it."

Shada stretched her awareness down to her hands. Over the years she'd spent a lot of time developing the grip and coordination of both to help in her sport, so she knew it was possible to bend just the last knuckle of her right pinky finger, if she could find it in the darkness.

"So there's no way she didn't let her body get turned on by the women just because she wasn't into women herself? It was her body's response?"

"Correct. Just because your mind wants something doesn't mean the body does. Interest and arousal aren't the same thing."

Hollis stared at the white wall as he digested the information. "If her body is aroused by men, then that means I'll have to use men for sexual satisfaction . . ."

"And if the thought is repulsive, then you'll just have to forego sexual stimulation," Alfie said.

Hollis exhaled and shook his head. At the same moment, Shada was able to find her hand and bend her pinky finger. She let go right away so Hollis wouldn't find out she was taking back control.

"Is there some sort of test we have to determine if she's

somehow still alive in here?" Hollis said, using one hand to gesture over the entirety of Shada's body.

Alfie pondered then shook his head. "Not that I'm aware of. We haven't had this problem in the others." Alfie took a rapid inhale and his eyes got wider; he'd said too much.

"Wait, there are others?"

"Yes, we've uploaded other edited minds into unedited bodies. A few hours at a time. You know that," Alfie said. He turned away in an effort to be dismissive.

"You said that like there are other permanent uploads. Are there?"

Alfie sighed. "You don't think we'd let the head of West-Corp be the first recipient of a new procedure, do you?"

CHAPTER TWENTY-FOUR

THE OTHER RECIPIENTS of permanent switches had never met before Hollis demanded their assembly. Two of them were brought in from the city, where their edited minds were trying to live in unedited bodies among the unedited. Alfie claimed this was for "research purposes" but never elaborated on what research was being conducted. Three other recipients of permanent switches resided on the island for observation. These were the first three WestCorp had ever produced, edited minds transplanted into edited bodies.

Hollis asked if these three maintained the same position within the company that their minds had occupied, or if the body's previous position was where they stayed. Alfie told him that all the uploaded minds had to stay at the level of the body so nobody would wonder how these people received their promotions.

Five other bodies, filled with five minds, and Shada wondered if any of the original minds were still active. She assumed they'd had enough time to find the light and could witness the world through their body's eyes, but she doubted they would be able to exert the level of control she had over her own body. It had taken her years of deliberate practice to learn how to control her body, and her level of body awareness was rare among athletes, let alone the general population.

Hollis-in-Shada walked through an empty warehouse to a small room in the back, one that could have been used as security but was now empty. It was identical to the room to which Piper had brought Shada and Chloe when they were offered the chance to receive the uploads in the first place. Alfie was already present with the other five, a pen and notebook in his lap. They were seated in a circle of chairs, waiting for Hollis-in-Shada to take the last available seat.

After Hollis sat down and nodded to Alfie, Alfie stood up and spoke.

"We've brought you together today because you six are the first ever edited consciousnesses transplanted into other bodies."

Everyone looked at the faces around them.

"Four of you reside here on the island for observation," Alfie said as he nodded to a broad-shouldered woman of Asian descent, a heavyset Caucasian man with a goatee and ponytail, a weasel of a man with stooped shoulders, then Shada. "And two of you have lived in the city." Alfie looked at a dark-haired man and woman with deep-set eyes who could have been related.

"I won't tell you what the name of everyone's previous body was, or their position, but trust me when I say all of you were once high-ranking officials in WestCorp."

The group looked at one another once more. Shada was curious about what the unedited humans did in the city, and where they lived, but she imagined the uploaded minds all brimmed with curiosity about the former identities of everyone around them, measuring where they might stack up.

"This is the first time we've brought the six of you together, and I'll have to ask that you not contact each other once we leave this room. Other than you two, of course." The two unedited bodies closed their eyes and nodded.

"What are we here for?" the Asian woman said. From the tone of her voice, and the way she felt entitled to an answer so early in the meeting, Shada guessed her mind came from a high-ranking male.

"Think of it as a support group. We want to hear about any issues you might have had so that others here can know what to expect. Not all of you have lived inside another body for so long, and some have found the experience jarring."

At the edge of her vision, Shada could see the man with the goatee look in her direction. She wondered if he had access to more information than the others.

"For those of you who now occupy a body different from your original gender, have you noticed a change in sexual desire?"

Alfie looked at each face in turn. Shada could have sworn he lingered on her face for just a moment longer.

Shada saw the Asian woman's hand raise and saw her own fingers lift while her hands still rested in her lap.

"What happened?"Alfie asked the Asian woman.

"Nothing at all, that's the problem! Women do nothing for me anymore! It's like looking at what I know should be my favorite food and not finding anything about it at all appetizing."

Alfie thanked her for sharing. "And with you?" he said to Hollis-in-Shada.

"Same thing here. I had two women over and there was zero enjoyment. It felt like I was witnessing two mammals, like something I'd see in a zoo. Purely scientific and rational. Completely ruined the experience for me."

"I can imagine it's quite a shock to realize something that brought you pleasure before has no effect on you anymore," Alfie said, nodding as he noted their responses.

Hollis-in-Shada and the Asian woman both nodded in agreement.

"Does anyone else have a similar experience?"

The members of the group all looked at one another before the unedited woman from the city spoke up. "I used to eat meat all the time, multiple meals a day. I knew this body ate a vegetarian diet before I took over, but I figured I would be able to still eat my normal foods. Turns out meat now makes me bloated and sluggish, so I've had to cut it out of my diet."

"Her gut microbiome wasn't prepared for the sudden introduction of meat," Alfie said, looking up and to the left as he riffed on the subject. "You could probably introduce meat slowly into your diet and over time get back to the levels you were at before. You have to give your body the chance the adjust."

"It's not even worth it," the unedited woman said. When she tucked her dark hair behind an ear, Shada wondered if this habit was one from her former edited self or if the body her mind now occupied did it on instinct. Of course, it could have been neither and the hair in front of her face was bothersome.

Over the next hour the group shared various quirks about life in their new bodies that they hadn't expected. Everyone had something to share, and things ranged from needing more sleep than before to a newfound sensation to engage in running as exercise.

During a lull in the conversation, Alfie placed both hands on his knees and leaned forward. "Does anyone have anything else they'd like to share? I'm going to schedule these sessions once a week, so if anything comes up, we can discuss the next time we meet."

The group was silent for a moment before Hollis-in-Shada spoke up. "Do any of you wonder what happened to the mind of the body we occupy? Like, it just sits in there? Are they dead? Could they take back over?"

The rest of the group seemed to look inwards before they directed their attention to Alfie for answers.

Alfie cleared his throat. "Their mind still exists, but it's trapped in a senseless void. The legal system clarified this position when they said the minds of those sentenced to life imprisonment, when uploaded into the body of someone from death row, continue to exist. The person on death row is considered dead."

"That's what the legal system says, but has there been any research on how complete the takeover actually is?"

"We've had no observed cases of the body's original mind taking back control. But this is an interesting topic, worthy of investigation. Let us know if there are any instances when you feel like you lose control so we can study the phenomenon."

"And what if it's discovered they are able to take back control? The prison system could cancel their contract with us and sue, costing us millions," the weasel said. He had the bearing of a man who thought in dollars and cents.

"Well, if we find anything, we just won't tell them," Alfie said, a mischievous glint in his eye.

CHAPTER TWENTY-FIVE

THE OLDER MALE secretary called into the leader's office and requested permission to enter.

"Come in," Hollis-in-Shada told him.

Shada wondered how much Ernie knew, or could guess, based on how she had been transformed into a VIP overnight. His ability to follow protocol with this upstart sitting in his boss's chair impressed her.

"I wanted to go over the details of your trip into the city tonight," Ernie said when he stood across the desk from Hollis-in-Shada.

"Go on."

Ernie laid a manila folder on the desk. "Hollis arranged for you to take the helicopter to city hall for a meeting." He handed Shada a single sheet of paper with the trip's itinerary laid out in bullet points. "You're scheduled to fly out at five, meet with a representative from five thirty to six thirty, and be back by seven. Does this all sound reasonable?"

Shada gained a unique satisfaction from the way the older man talked to her. This would be her first ride in a helicopter, although without sensations from her body, the ride would be more like watching a scene from a movie than an experience. She knew she must have seen this in an action movie at some point in her life but couldn't recall a specific example.

"It all sounds reasonable to me. What will this meeting be about?" Hollis-in-Shada asked.

Shada hoped this wasn't a test by Hollis. She liked Ernie and wanted him to stick around.

Ernie looked apprehensive, the first time he seemed unsure about how much information to divulge. "Hollis never told me what you'll be meeting about, but every other time he's visited, an announcement followed about our technology being used by the city's government."

"Like . . ." Hollis-in-Shada said.

"I'll let them tell you more. I'd imagine Hollis has already briefed them about what you will be talking about. If I had to guess though, it has something to do with your recent uploads."

So Ernie knew Shada had been uploaded into. Shada doubted the meeting had anything to do with her specific experience but appreciated the innocence with which he made the suggestion. It seemed like he was trying his best to find common ground, to include Shada to the best of his ability, but without clear direction from Hollis, his fear of giving the unedited woman too much information held his tongue.

Hollis gathered the papers back into the manila folder and placed it next to his keyboard.

"Did you want Beth to get you anything to eat for the trip?" Ernie asked.

"I already have my meals, but . . . I've got a strange craving for candy. Something sweet and chewy. Could you have her find something in the food court and bring it to me for dessert?" Hollis said.

Shada was proud her body still craved those red gummy bears Sikya hated so much.

Right before it was time for the helicopter to depart, Beth showed up with multiple options of chewy candy. None of them were Shada's old favorite. Hollis-in-Shada selected a single bag of candied peach rings, carried them across the concrete landing pad, then boarded the craft. The bag was empty by the time they landed on the roof of city hall.

A man in a blue suit with an earpiece in one ear stood next to a door that jutted out from a corner of the roof. He gestured for Hollis-in-Shada to come to him. The wind generated by the helicopter's rotors made words useless, so Hollis tapped the back of the pilot's chair twice before he jumped out and ran towards the door.

The suited man's black hair, parted on the side, stood as solid against the wind as his flexed jaw. He held the door open for what he perceived was a woman, gesturing with his head for Hollis-in-Shada to go through first. On the other side of the door was a handsome set of dark brown circular stairs with an elegant railing on both sides. When the door shut behind them, blocking the noise of the helicopter, the man urged Hollis-in-Shada to head down.

"There will be someone waiting for you," he said, all business.

The stairs ended in a waiting room outside the mayor's office. A middle-aged woman with red hair and yellowed teeth sat at a desk outside a pair of double doors with cameras above.

"Good afternoon," the woman said with a close-lipped smile. "I'll tell Mayor Fitzgerald you've arrived."

Although the secretary urged Hollis-in-Shada to sit, Hollis remained standing and looked at historical pictures from the construction of city hall on the room's walls. He lingered on one that showed the laying of the building's cornerstone. It showed a past mayor without a suit jacket, sleeves rolled up and a construction hat on, leaning against a shovel surrounded by numerous construction workers.

"The mayor is ready for you," the secretary said.

Hollis tore his eyes away from the picture, nodded to the woman behind the desk, and walked through the double doors.

The mayor, a small bald man with circular glasses, stood up and shook hands with Hollis-in-Shada. "James," he said with a smile.

"Shada," Hollis replied. "I trust you've been told that I'm here representing Hollis?"

The smile disappeared from the mayor's face. "I was informed."

"Then let's get to it," Hollis said.

The mayor directed Hollis-in-Shada to a sofa and two matching chairs on one side of his office. "Care for anything to drink?" he said, gesturing to a small bar.

"No thanks," Hollis replied. He sat down on the couch, and the mayor sat on a chair.

The mayor informed Hollis-in-Shada that the plan was coming along well. He kept telling his guest that her boss would be pleased with the progress.

Hollis launched into a description of the plan, which Shada assumed was to demonstrate to the mayor how informed his guest was. "Since you seem to be skirting around the specifics, I'll give you a sense of my level of involvement. I know you have been denying birth licenses to all unedited humans who don't plan on editing their children pre-birth."

The mayor waited for Hollis-in-Shada to continue.

"WestCorp will offer post-birth edits at reduced rates for those who are denied birth licenses multiple times. These will be marketed as a fix to their biological clock, a chance through science to be content without having children. These reduced rates haven't been rolled out yet. Nobody has recognized the mass denials, as far as we know, and the purpose of this meeting is to see if there has been any recognition among the unedited of their new reality."

Shada knew Sikya was a victim of this plan.

The mayor leaned forward in his chair and rested his hands on his knees. "That's where Hollis and I left things last time he was here."

"So has there been any news?"

"There have been a few grumblings by those who want to have unedited children, but receiving post-birth edits isn't on their radar, as far as I know. They want to have unregistered children."

"Is that even possible?"

"In theory, yes, but they'd be kicked out of the city. Not many people are willing to risk the wilderness to have a child."

"So these grumblings are pointless." Hollis-in-Shada leaned back on the sofa and stared at the ceiling.

"For the most part. The lawsuits are still trickling in."

"Good. We'll wait until they're desperate before we announce the cheaper post-birth edits as a solution to their frustration."

Shada felt helpless knowing there was no way to communicate with her sister. If she could, she would tell her not to fall for the trap and to alert the people she knew who fought for unedited rights. She reached for her breath in order to calm down, not caring if Hollis discovered her control.

Hollis was too busy formulating ways to make the unedited people even more desperate in order to speed the process along to notice the change in breathing. He was insistent WestCorp be seen as the great savior from the evil City's government, with promises of increased funding for the mayor and the city.

"We haven't seen any money yet," the mayor complained.

"Your money will come once people begin post-birth edits. That's what we agreed on."

"Hollis said all of the money from the post-birth edits will come to us." The mayor shifted in his seat. "My only question is, why does WestCorp care if people edit themselves post-birth if they won't make any money on it?"

"Because, mayor, within a generation we can rid the city of all unedited humans once and for all."

CHAPTER TWENTY-SIX

THE MAYOR HAD a fruit and cheese plate brought in, and between bites he reported on other business ventures WestCorp was involved in with the city. The life sentences of prisoners, increased advertising, and better transportation options for WestCorp employees still living in the city were all discussed with minimal awareness on Shada's part as to what was being said.

Shada couldn't stop thinking about how WestCorp wanted to force all humans to be edited, to annihilate the unedited population—not right away and not against their will, but by making them suffer so much they gave up the part of themselves that made them human.

By the end of the meeting, Hollis-in-Shada had demonstrated such intimate knowledge of WestCorp's inner workings that the mayor seemed to be at total ease with his guest. "You'll fill Hollis in on all we've talked about today, right?"

"That's correct," Hollis-in-Shada said.

Shada saw her hand rise to display a small electrical device the size of a thumbnail. "This has been recording our entire conversation. I'll have him listen to it when I get back to the island."

"It's too bad he couldn't be here today, but I'm glad to have gotten the chance to get to know you," the mayor said. He switched seats and sat next to Hollis-in-Shada on the couch.

Shada had been around men long enough to know when their minds transitioned to their base instincts. She doubted Hollis knew the signs.

The mayor leaned in close, and Shada could smell the cheese on his breath. This was the first time she'd smelled anything since before the hijack. The scent thrilled her even though she had a sense of how repulsed she would be if she were in control of her body. The smell of the rest of the room flooded her awareness, and she was aware of the faint smell of glass cleaning solution, of musty carpet, and stale cologne. With the addition of a sense of smell came a greater awareness of her body. She was convinced she could move her entire arm if she wanted.

Hollis wasn't aware of the mayor's intentions until his hand fell on Hollis-in-Shada's leg. Hollis scrambled away. "What are you doing?" he said in Shada's voice.

The mayor wasn't deterred by the reaction. "Now that business is over, how about a little pleasure? This isn't the first time Hollis has sent a woman over."

Shada took control of her body and punched the mayor in the face. Hollis stared at Shada's hand for a moment before launching into a tirade. "Did any of those women ever talk to you about business? Get your head out of your ass, I am—" Hollis grew quiet.

The mayor rubbed his cheek and smiled. "You're what?" he asked.

Hollis-in-Shada stood up. "Leaving," Hollis said. He left the office, ignored the secretary, and began the climb back up to the roof.

Shada found joy in knowing her face would forever be attributed to punching the mayor's face, even if it was just between the two of them. Little did the mayor know that all of his future dealings with "Hollis" would be with her. She felt a prickle of awareness as Hollis grasped in the dark for her.

He had to know she was inside and could guess it was her who threw the punch.

Shada tried to retreat, but when she pulled back her own awareness, the hand she had taken control of to punch the mayor froze. It now served two masters. The hand was about to grasp the rail, and without the support, Hollis-in-Shada stumbled on the stairs.

"I knew it!" Hollis screamed in Shada's voice.

Shada tried her best to retreat, and even lost awareness of her body's breathing, but the hand remained motionless.

Hollis stared at the hand, trying to get it to move. He slammed it against the wall then banged it on the railing. It didn't reanimate. Desperate, he sandwiched his right index finger between the thumb and palm edge of his right hand. "I'll break it," he said.

Shada thought it strange that he threatened her with damage to a body that no longer belonged to her. In a surge of focus, she took back control of her breath and stopped his next inhale.

When Hollis realized he couldn't breathe, he looked around the stairwell as if his attacker could be on the ceiling. The right index finger was released, and Shada took back full control of the hand. She pointed her index finger and shook it from side to side, telling Hollis no. She allowed her body to breathe again.

Hollis used the left hand to support himself on the railing and gulped air. While he was preoccupied with breathing again,

Shada took over the rest of her body. She stood up straight, breathed twice through her nose, and said to the air around her, "How does it feel?"

She climbed the stairs and prepared to head back to the island to destroy Hollis's work.

When she reached the top of the stairs, she realized Hollis had taken control of her breathing. He was using the same method to take back control that she had used to find control in the first place. He stopped her breathing and Shada fell to the ground.

Hollis stood Shada's body up, back in control, and opened the door. The helicopter pilot spotted him and turned on the rotors. Hollis rushed past the security guard with the stationary hair as the craft came alive.

Shada had allowed Hollis into her body so Sikya could have a child. Hollis would stand by that statement, he would allow Sikya to have a child, so long as it was edited before birth. A condition Sikya wouldn't agree to.

Shada wanted revenge.

Hollis didn't make it halfway to the helicopter before Shada was able to take back control. In that moment, she decided to destroy Hollis once and for all. Her body veered to the left, and she forced herself to walk towards the edge of the roof but was stopped when Hollis stopped their body in its tracks.

On the roof of city hall, two consciousnesses took turns controlling different parts of the same body, one with the goal of jumping off the roof and the other wanting to board the helicopter. To those witnessing the struggle, it looked like two stop-motion animations had become interwoven.

It became clear Shada was winning the fight, because her body kept inching closer to the edge of the roof. In a rare moment of near-complete control, Shada was able to use one leg to hop towards the edge while Hollis used the other as an anchor. She was able to win because she fought not only for herself but for her sister and future niece or nephew. She was convinced if she could kill Hollis, she could save them all.

Shada was tackled a few steps from the edge of the roof. She saw the blue suit of the security guard on top of her.

"Tie me in and take me to Alfie," Shada heard herself say.

Shada continued to struggle, but the guard was trained to manipulate those who resisted.

The guard looked confused but relayed her words to the pilot. He nodded in understanding before the two of them tied Shada to one of the rear-facing chairs in the helicopter and they took off.

Over the bay, Shada discovered that as long as she stayed in control of her breathing, she could trap Hollis inside for good.

CHAPTER TWENTY-SEVEN

SHADA WAS LEFT in the helicopter while the pilot ran to get reinforcements. Through the headset covering her ears she could hear the blades overhead slowing down. The waves of the bay rolled into shore while Shada focused on her breathing. She could feel Hollis fighting to regain control, but she didn't allow any space for him to find footing in her diaphragm.

The pilot returned with Alfie and two security guards. By then Shada was covered in sweat from the heat inside the black helicopter. Alfie removed the headset from over Shada's ears and asked, "How do you feel?"

"I feel fine," Shada said, trying to mimic the impatient way Hollis sounded when he spoke with her voice.

"The pilot said you had an episode before takeoff."

"I did. Not sure what happened, but I'm back to normal now." Shada attempted her best commanding tone. "Untie me."

Alfie gave her a quizzical look. "I will, but we're going to have to go to the lab for an assessment."

Shada continued her impression of Hollis. "That won't be necessary. I have a lot of work to do, no time for assessments." She didn't pay as much attention to her breathing; her efforts were spent impersonating Hollis instead. In the space that opened up, Hollis grabbed hold of a breath before Shada forced him back into the darkness.

Hollis's attempt to take back control showed up to Alfie as a startled gasp. "What's wrong?" he asked, now on high alert.

"Nothing, nothing," Shada said. "The heat is getting to me."

Alfie flashed a knowing smile before he untied Shada. He instructed the two massive guards to accompany them to his office. "Each of you place a hand on one of her shoulders; I don't want another episode of what happened on the roof."

Alfie thanked the pilot, telling him that he'd done well in making sure Shada was secure on the return trip, before dismissing him.

The party of four took a transport vehicle back to the atrium and walked through, the guards flanking Shada the entire time, before they ended up in Alfie's office. He told the two guards to stand outside.

"Take a seat on the table," Alfie said to Shada when they were alone.

"Really, I'm fine. This isn't necessary," Shada said.

Alfie looked at her, a stern look beneath raised eyebrows, and Shada acquiesced. She climbed onto the table and looked down at her hands. Still aware of every breath, she flexed each finger joint in turn, starting with her right pinky finger and working her way to the left. Meanwhile, Alfie pulled up both her file and Hollis's on the computer before sitting down on his circular stool on wheels.

Alfie took a quick trip through Shada's major joints, asking her to move each one. Ankles, knees, hips, then shoulders, elbows, and wrists. After Shada demonstrated control of each, Alfie asked if she felt any of them were slow to respond.

"Nope," Shada said. "Everything seems to be working fine." She impressed herself at how much she was able to invoke

Hollis in her voice this time, sounding both exasperated and commanding at the same time.

"Do you have any concern that your host was able to take back control? Or was fighting for control?" Alfie asked. His pen hovered over the file in his hand.

"You mean because of the incident on the roof? I wanted to look at the city from above and stumbled on my way over, that's all." Shada continued to count her breaths in the background.

"The pilot said it was more than a stumble. He said it looked like you were fighting against yourself. His words. And the last time you were in here, we were talking about your concern that the host was able to take back control. Now, I didn't witness the event, but it sounds like you were fighting to keep control of this body."

Shada tilted her head to the side. "I can see how it could look like that, but I'm telling you I'm fine!"

Alfie jotted something down in the file before looking back at her. "And tell me how you feel."

"I feel great," Shada said. She lowered her chin. "Ready to get back to all the work I have," she growled.

"In time, in time. I understand this is frustrating, sir, but this is important. The pilot swore you were going to jump off the roof. You tell me, does this sound like someone who is fine?"

"It does when I'm telling you I am."

"OK, OK. There's just one more thing we have to do." Alfie stood up and withdrew a modified helmet from a cabinet on the wall.

Shada watched as Alfie plugged it into the computer. She didn't want to ask what he was going to do, because she didn't want her ignorance of the procedure to tip him off that Hollis was no longer in control. She tried to come up with possible uses for the device, wondering if there was a chance her consciousness would be pulled out and placed back inside.

If this was the case, should she leave Hollis inside and hope her body would stay unconscious until she returned?

Or should she allow Hollis to be withdrawn by allowing him to take back control at the last possible moment, so he could be pulled into the machine while she stayed in her own body? She wasn't sure she would be able to relinquish control on command, in which case it would be a coin flip to see which of them would be withdrawn.

While she tried both these options on for size, she counted her ten breaths over and over again in order to keep Hollis at bay. Alfie asked her to lie down, and Shada wondered if Hollis had learned to see through her eyes. She doubted it.

Alfie explained the process as he placed the helmet on Shada's head. "Since our last discussion I've been thinking about how to measure if the host is able to control any body processes, and I think I've come up with a way to measure. Before we can transplant consciousness, we have to scan the mind that will be transplanted. That's really what this device does," he pulled the helmet straps tight. "Creates a map. What I'll do is create a new map of your mind and look for inconsistencies in the connections between neurons. If the host has taken back control of anything, they should show up as dark spots."

"Will I be unconscious?"

"No, you'll be awake the whole time. The only way you can lose consciousness is if there is another body to switch into, but since none are hooked up, there's nowhere to go." Computer keys clicked as Shada waited for the scan to begin. "OK, lie still. This will take a few minutes," Alfie said.

Shada took extra care to focus on the exhale of each of her next ten breaths. She began a second round and got to two more exhales before Alfie said the scan was complete.

"Any inconsistencies?" Shada asked.

Alfie stared at the screen, his head blocking Shada's view. He searched every corner, and when his head moved, Shada could see a series of white dots with thin white lines stretched between them. He nodded his head. "I don't see any dark spots," he said. He sounded surprised, as if he'd expected some part of another's consciousness to show up on the screen.

"So I can take this thing off?"

Alfie rolled over and helped Shada take off the headgear.

"So I can go?" Shada asked.

"Yes, sir. Sorry to hold you for so long, but I had to be sure."

When Alfie said "sir," Shada remembered she'd forgotten to talk as if she was Hollis. The leader of WestCorp would never ask to go; he'd inform Alfie that he was leaving. She stood up and walked out of the room, hoping the scientist didn't notice that something about the end of their interaction wasn't quite right.

CHAPTER TWENTY-EIGHT

SHADA STARED at Hollis's computer while she sat in the high-backed chair behind his desk. She had memorized his password, so getting into the system wasn't a problem, but she had no idea how to begin the large-scale sabotage she envisioned.

It was the morning after her trip into the city, and she had woken up in a panic, worried Hollis had been able to take back control of her body. After a quick body scan and a series of purposeful breaths, she knew she was still the one in charge, though she sensed Hollis in the background. She guessed that as long as she was asleep, Hollis had no sensations to ground his attempt to retake control.

Shada clicked on various folders and stumbled upon files for every employee at WestCorp. At first, she clicked random names and checked to see how much money they made, but she stopped once she realized the information was useless to her. She opened his email and couldn't find a single reference to his plan with the mayor for the city's unedited inhabitants.

She had no idea where the sensitive files were. Even if she had, she wasn't sure whether she should corrupt them, delete them, or send them away to some outside entity who would be able to exact revenge.

"The movies make it look so easy," she said to herself.

She gave up her quest for a smoking gun and stared at the bay through the window. Waves continued to roll onto the island; their perpetual motion made Shada realize her attempts to subvert WestCorp would be like trying to stop the tide. No matter what happened they would keep coming, and the only way to end them once and for all would be to remove their source.

The source was trapped inside her.

She knew she could keep Hollis trapped, but only as long as she kept control of each and every breath she took. This was no way to live a life. Something in the depths of the water called out to her, and she knew she had to follow through on the plan she'd first come up with on the roof. Hollis must be killed, and the only way to do it would involve sacrificing herself.

Ernie called into the office in the middle of Shada's daydream about the best way to kill herself. Shada put him on speaker and was informed Alfie was there to see her.

"Send him in," Shada said. She felt like Alfie was on her turf now, even though the office belonged to Hollis.

Alfie walked in, followed by Chloe. Based on her lack of recognition, Shada guessed her friend's body was occupied by another person's consciousness.

Shada did her best to avoid the eyes of her friend, reminding herself that Hollis would have no reason to care about this random unedited person. This preoccupation almost made her lose track of her breath. Shada sensed Hollis at the periphery of her awareness, waiting for the opportunity to retake control.

"I wanted you to see the first person uploaded into four times," Alfie said from behind Chloe. He placed a hand on her shoulder and beamed with pride. "Your host was friends with her."

Shada leaned back in her chair and assumed a nonchalant air as she played along. "Four times? Has she shown any signs of degradation?"

"I'll let her answer that," Alfie said, turning to a stone-faced Chloe. "Did you notice any resistance? Does there seem to be any lag?" Alfie asked.

Chloe squeezed her lips together and shook her head. "Seems like every other time," she responded.

"Her body accepted the upload at the same rate as before," Alfie added.

Shada stood up and walked around the desk to where Chloe and Alfie stood. She circled Chloe, assuming Hollis would do the same if he was in control. Chloe was smiling when Shada returned to her front.

"Is it really you?" Chloe said.

Shada was surprised by the question. She looked at Alfie for direction, wondering if this could be Chloe taking back control. Nothing in the scientist's face suggested he was worried. All he did was smile.

"It's really me," Shada said to Chloe, trying her best to sound confident. She was herself, after all.

"I always knew you could do it. Interesting choice of body though," Chloe said. It was her turn to inspect the other, and her eyes went from head to toe and back again.

Shada shot Alfie a look that asked, "Does she know?"

"I told her," Alfie said with a nod.

Confused, Shada withdrew into counting her breaths in order to maintain her composure.

"Are you OK?" Chloe asked.

"I'm fine. I've found that focused breathing keeps me grounded," Shada said. She hoped somewhere inside Chloe's body her friend heard her words and would reach for these important first steps of taking back control.

"Who do you think this is?" Chloe asked Shada.

"I'm . . . I'm not sure," Shada replied. Alfie's knowing smile tempted her to punch him in the face.

Chloe brushed Shada's cheek with the back of her hand. "It's Ruby."

Shada had no idea who Ruby was, but she knew the response this type of touch should elicit. She also knew edited humans didn't feel attachments to the same degree as the unedited, so she felt she could delay an emotional response in favor of a rational one.

"What were you thinking?" Shada said to Alfie.

"Relax, it's just me," Ruby-in-Chloe said.

"She's the only one I told," Alfie explained. "I told her before she uploaded."

"I made him tell me!" Ruby-in-Chloe said. "When I heard about the incident on the roof, I got worried. Alfie said we should upload my mind into this girl and see your response. I think he fears your host was able to take back control."

Alfie glared at Chloe. "You weren't supposed to tell him that."

"Oh, what does it matter? You said he passed the inspection in your office."

"And this was another test. Worthless, now."

Shada returned to her chair on the far side of the desk and left the two visitors standing.

"Make sure you let me know how the host does once the procedure has been reversed," Shada said, dismissing them.

"Of course," Alfie replied.

"I'll come see you in my own skin," Ruby-in-Chloe said.

"Don't bother, I have lots of work to do," Shada said. She was pleased to see Chloe's face fall at the dismissal.

Alfie guided Chloe towards the door. Before he left, he told Shada the report about Chloe's condition post-upload would be sent over that afternoon.

Alone again in the office, Shada returned to the computer and looked up Ruby. There were three individuals on the company payroll with that first name, but one of their last names was Hollis. Shada clicked on the file and began to read.

She discovered Ruby Hollis was Michael Hollis's wife. Still married, but separate primary residences. Her birth date made her the same approximate age as the leader of WestCorp, but the photo attached to the file showed a middle-aged woman instead of the advanced age that would be expected. The file didn't reference a date of marriage; instead, a date of assignment was listed from when Hollis was thirty. Two arrival dates were listed, one year and three years after their assignment, and Shada assumed these corresponded to the birth dates of their children.

Shada typed out a message to Alfie telling him to kill Ruby when the upload was reversed. She wondered if the message, without justification, would be enough for Alfie to follow through with the orders. If Alfie was convinced Hollis was still in control, he might have listened, but the lingering doubt he harbored, evidenced by testing Shada with Chloe's body, made Shada think the orders wouldn't be carried out.

Shada deleted the message. One Hollis death would be enough to make her happy.

CHAPTER TWENTY-NINE

ALFIE ASKED SHADA, assuming it was Hollis, to come to his office. "There's something I have to show you in person," he said. He wouldn't elaborate over the phone, regardless of Shada's insistence.

Shada guessed Hollis would resist going to Alfie's office—it would have something to do with power dynamics, she was sure —and might even make the scientist wait until the next day, but her curiosity got the best of her, so she agreed to the meeting. She assumed it was about Chloe.

Alfie's office was flanked by two security guards. Shada walked in, unannounced, the way she imagined Hollis might do. She caught Alfie seated at his desk, deep in thought. The faraway look of a man whose thoughts are somewhere else evaporated when his eyes focused on her, replaced by a deep fatigue set in darkened eye sockets. On his desk was a grid of eight vials, standing vertical in two rows of four.

"Please take a seat," Alfie said, gesturing to the chair opposite him.

Shada told Alfie she had been sitting all day and would rather stand. She wondered if Hollis would ever do the same.

"I need to give you an injection," Alfie said, not wasting any time.

"An injection? What for?"

"I designed this to keep your host from taking back control. It took me all night." He withdrew one of the vials and rolled it between his fingers.

Shada weighed her options. Hollis, fearful of Shada, would accept the injection without question in order to keep her consciousness under his thumb. Shada knew she was in control at the moment, but for how long? If this injection served to keep him silent, then she could have Alfie continue production for her to use it long-term, allowing her to eliminate Hollis without killing herself.

The injection seemed like a good idea.

Shada sat down and laid her bare arm over Alfie's desk. Alfie withdrew a needle and syringe from a desk drawer and injected the clear liquid. He gave her a cotton swab to hold over the injection site.

"Give it a few minutes to kick in," Alfie said, exhausted.

"What was it?" Shada asked.

"A modified form of LSD. It makes the subconscious conscious."

Shada's eyes got wide, and she stared at Alfie. The scientist seemed to be carrying a massive weight on his shoulders that didn't allow him to sit up straight in his chair.

"I thought you said it would help keep him under control . . ."

She realized too late that she'd said him.

Alfie closed his eyes and exhaled. "I had a feeling you were back," he said. "I wanted to have a conversation with whoever's in the background. I'm not sure it will work, but I didn't know what else to do."

Shada felt strings of panic pull her down and focused on her

149

exhale.

"I had a feeling before I brought Chloe over with Ruby trapped inside. She ruined the test by telling you, but I still couldn't shake the thought. Hollis and Ruby were never close—edited relationships are different from what you're used to in the city—but there was nothing to suggest you even recognized the personality of the woman you were paired with for over two decades."

Shada felt reality slipping away from her, and counting breaths did nothing to slow its departure. Hollis was coming back and there was nothing she could do about it. It wasn't the same as before, when one had control and the other had to sit in the background. It was more like they both shared the same space, two halves of the brain who had access to one body. For now she could keep her mouth shut, but she wasn't sure for how long.

Alfie didn't seem to care about Shada's silence. He continued telling Shada how he'd arrived at his conclusion.

"I came back into my office after Ruby left Chloe's body—both women are fine, by the way—and took a look at the mapping of your neurons. I was looking for the dark spots, certain I had missed something. It didn't even occur to me that you, Shada, would be able to take back complete control. But then it hit me. Why would Hollis know how to control parts of his body that weren't his? Once he lost control, it would be the most natural thing in the world for you to shut him out. That's why there weren't any dark spots."

Alfie turned his computer monitor around and rested an elbow on his desk. The screen showed two images side by side, each a series of white dots connected by thin white lines. They were the same type of picture, but it didn't take a scientist to know they were different. Alfie pointed to the one on the left.

"This is the map we made last night. Notice no dark spots?

This is why I assumed there was no loss of control."

Shada tried to nod but ended up jerking her head left and right.

"The one on the right is a map I had of Hollis's brain from his initial upload. We don't have a map of your brain; well, we didn't before last night. I think it's clear these two aren't the same. Now, the way the uploads work is that we take one neural mapping and transpose it onto another brain. There are paths of least resistance present, from the previous occupant, but the machine we designed is able to highlight these connections and negate them, while amplifying the correct ones, allowing the upload to take hold. Imagine it like this: we are able to turn on and up every neuron and connection in a brain, making it into a block of marble. Then we chisel away the necessary parts to sculpt the statue we are trying to create."

Shada put her head in her hands and tried to focus on her breath.

"That's all a mind is, a series of firing neurons and their connections. Right now, we have the ability to copy one map onto another, but in time we hope to design our own minds from scratch. In a robot, this would be called artificial intelligence. In a human, we call it the Vitruvian Man."

Shada lost control of her breathing. The drug didn't make her hallucinate, which she'd expected, but instead allowed her to feel a connection to the world around her, a sense of wonder that allowed her to view Alfie not just as a person but as a wonderful example of life. The wood of his desk seemed to call out to her, its smooth edges a marvel of human ingenuity. Without a firm hold of reality, Hollis took back control.

"That bitch tried to kill me!" Hollis-in-Shada said. The words didn't come out in one smooth statement but between facial spasms.

Alfie displayed a tired smile. "Welcome back, sir."

CHAPTER THIRTY

"You're going to pay for that one," Hollis said to Shada's reflection in the bathroom mirror. He was back in his underground bunker after spending the last few days under Alfie's direct supervision. Together they'd determined how often the low-dose LSD had to be administered in order for Hollis to maintain control over Shada's body. One injection every fifteen hours was the minimum, but they shortened the window to twelve hours to be on the safe side.

Hollis stared at what was now his reflection and made a show of holding his breath. His cheeks puffed out, and he put his hand on his throat, holding onto his air for so long his face turned red. His loud exhale was followed by a maniacal laugh.

"There's nothing you can do!" he said.

Shada didn't try to retake control of her body's breathing. There were a few times during Alfie's observation when she thought it might be possible, but a new dose of the drug would take away her ability to focus. It would create a sense of wonder and appreciation for the world around her, a content sensation that snapped away from her as soon as Hollis retook control. She went through this cycle of attraction and repulsion to retaking control a few times before she gave up. Now she stayed in the background, watching and hearing the world through what used to be her eyes and ears.

Hollis disclosed to Alfie that he'd had no sensations while Shada maintained control. He never knew where he was and couldn't hear a thing. He said it was like being in a dark room, alone with his thoughts.

Shada thought forever in solitude would be a fitting end for such a despicable human.

Hollis pried himself away from the bathroom mirror and went into the kitchen. He withdrew one of the premade meals and began to eat it cold.

"I'm not sure you can hear me, but I'm going to pretend you can," he said through a full mouth.

Alfie and Hollis had never gotten Shada to speak about her experience being trapped inside her own body. They assumed she experienced it the same way as Hollis but couldn't be sure.

"Your sister, I forget her name, hasn't received a cent."

Shada knew her blood would boil if she had access to a body.

"And it's your fault. The transfer was set up, but we wanted to wait to make sure the upload was permanent. You can thank Piper for that idea. There's a phrase I had to say to Alfie, but you took back control so soon I never said it."

Hollis stopped chewing and stared at the cavern above, listening for a response that would never come.

"Are you curious about what the phrase is?" Hollis took another bite and listened once more.

"Well, you'll have to stay curious, because I'm not going to tell you. What if you are able to retake control?"

Hollis shoveled food into Shada's mouth, not taking any extra time to chew. "You only have yourself to blame," he said.

Shada knew she couldn't kill herself, and therefore Hollis,

before Sikya received the money. If she did, it would make the hijack pointless. There had to be a way for her to take back control, but even if she did, she wouldn't know the phrase.

The shores of hope, once in sight, had disappeared, and she was left alone to drift in the sea.

She thought back to when she'd had control of Hollis and was alone with access to his computer. She hadn't even thought to check on Sikya. What kind of sister was she? Even if Sikya never got the windfall Hollis had promised, Shada could have done something, even if it was just sending a message telling her she was all right.

She had a long time to come to grips with the oversight.

Hollis finished his meal and threw away the silverware along with the disposable container. He walked back into the bathroom and opened the bathroom mirror, exposing shelves empty except for a small box of razors. From the box he withdrew a single razor blade and left the rest of the box next to the sink.

Hollis closed the mirror and leaned forward, leaving Shada's face an inch from the surface. Her eyes were so close that the flecks of black inside her brown irises were easy to distinguish.

"I want you to cry for your sister," Hollis said.

Shada watched her own hand, a razor squeezed between her thumb and forefinger, rise to her face and hover just below her right eye. Her own lips parted in a grin as the corner of the blade pressed against the lower part of her eye socket and continued straight down until even with the base of her nose. The parting of the red sea recreated in flesh.

Hollis admired his handiwork.

"I spent a lot of time thinking of ways to punish you. As an athlete, you prize your body. But now that this body belongs to me, anything I do to it would just be a punishment for me too!

But then I thought how useless this pretty face is. Anything, or anyone, I want, I can afford to buy myself."

Hollis stared at Shada's reflection for a moment before bringing the razor up to her left eye. "I'm a sucker for symmetry," he said as he repeated the procedure on the other side of her face.

Blood dripped from the two wounds. Each drop strengthened Shada's resolve to make Hollis pay.

"Wipe away those crocodile tears!" Hollis said. Shada couldn't tell if he was angry or joking. He contorted Shada's mouth into a dramatic frown and stammered, "But my sister!" then slammed a fist onto the counter.

He looked down. Drops of blood joined previous neighbors, pooled together, and covered the sink's edges. Hollis made no attempt to move Shada's head so the blood dripped closer to the drain. He lifted Shada's head enough to see the tops of her eyes.

"You did this to yourself," he said.

CHAPTER THIRTY-ONE

THE WOUNDS on Shada's face required stitches, but Hollis didn't address them. He went about the rest of his day as if nothing had happened, ignoring the pain. The few times he caught his reflection in the mirror, he smiled at the gashes. When he did, the corners of Shada's eyes crinkled up and distorted the straight lines running down her cheeks. Hollis didn't seem to register the pain, or if he did, he enjoyed it.

In bed that night, without any bandaging, the open wound on his right cheek scabbed over and became fused with the pillow. When Hollis opened his eyes the next morning, he couldn't lift his head.

Shada, her consciousness bathed in darkness while Hollis slept, became aware of the room as soon as her body's eyes opened. She couldn't feel her face attached to the pillow, but when Hollis cursed, she knew something was wrong.

Hollis began to count. "One...two..." he said in her own voice.

On the count of three Hollis ripped his face from the pillow. Shada's right hand rose up, touched her right cheek, and came away covered in blood.

Hollis didn't inspect the damage. Instead, he went into the kitchen and devoured the day's first meal.

Alfie came over to administer the day's first dose. Their agreed-upon schedule was eight in the morning and eight at night. Shada could tell, but she wasn't sure Hollis recognized, that Alfie did his best to avoid looking at her face.

"Any adverse effects?" Alfie asked as he withdrew the needle from Shada's arm.

Hollis shook his head. "Haven't heard from her since the first injection."

"That's good. What happened to your face?"

"Oh, these? I just wanted to decorate," Hollis said.

"Decorate your face?"

"What, you don't like what I've done?"

"Sir, let me remind you that this is your body now. Any harm you do must be considered self-harm. With this treatment's potential for psychosis, it will have to be reevaluated."

"No!" Hollis yelled. "I'm fine. I did this so she would see who's in charge now," he said with disgust.

"There's no doubt about that anymore." Alfie said, exasperated. "We'll continue the injections, but I'll be looking for alternatives. In the meantime, don't show your host who's in charge again. I'm worried you'll go too far."

"Like you said, it's my body. If I ruin this one, I can always get another."

"You can't think like that. The further you get from your own body, the greater the chance of degradation. You are in charge, you don't have to show her."

Hollis thought while Alfie gathered up his trash and threw it away.

"Why don't you bring some girls over here tonight? I'm sure she won't like that."

Alfie turned towards Hollis-in-Shada and looked at him with crestfallen eyes. "I can do that."

"Two. Young."

"They'll be with me when I come back for your evening injection."

Hollis waved Alfie away. With the scientist gone, he went into his study. His day was spent behind his computer, working from home, looking over his company's operations.

Shada was too busy trying to take back control to pay attention to his work. Each time she tried to focus on her breath, which had worked so well before, she would be struck by a disorienting sense of wonder at the world around her. She felt connected to the environment, as if she could sense the life that once was in this underground chamber. She couldn't decide which physical form the life took, which creatures were killed or driven out by the creation of Hollis's residence, but knew that the enormous length of time it had existed held a certain power. Her focus was drawn away in this fashion every time she tried to take back control of her breathing, meaning she never succeeded in holding on for more than a moment. It was like trying to pull herself from dark water by clawing at slippery rocks, never gaining enough traction to lift herself out but not losing herself inside its depths.

Shada was shocked at how young the two girls Alfie brought back with him were. They couldn't have been more than teenagers. She thought to herself how wrong this was and wondered what perverse intentions Hollis had for them. How would he show Shada who was in charge?

The girls watched Alfie administer the second injection of the day, all four of them seated at the expansive kitchen table. When Alfie left, they sat still, awaiting instruction.

Shada felt the increased awareness of the world around her

that came with the drug's administration, the strange wonder at all living things. These two girls in the room with her, they had their whole lives ahead of them. An awareness of their beating hearts informed her they were unedited, and she was filled with an overwhelming sense of connection with their vitality. As Shada listened, the two girls' hearts began to beat in sync.

All of this occurred in the time in which Hollis inspected his companions.

From deep within the cavern of her consciousness, Shada felt a sense of her own heartbeat synchronizing with those of the two young girls. The resonation of the three hearts reverberated off the cavern's walls. If she took a second to think about what she sensed, she would decide it wasn't possible by the laws of physics for any of these feelings to be proven, nullifying their power. She ignored rationality and maintained the awareness of life in both herself and the room.

Shada focused on her own heartbeat and found a sense of peace. At the same moment, Hollis instructed the teenagers to take off their clothes.

The two girls stood up and began to disrobe.

Shada focused on her own heartbeat and felt her awareness travel alongside her blood to every corner of her body. It began in her chest and spread out, down to her toes and up to the crown of her head. She felt herself swallow hard, Hollis's doing, and realized she could control her mouth. Not because she'd trapped Hollis deep inside, but because she accepted his attempts at control and decided not to allow them. Like wanting to eat but deciding to skip the meal, aware of hunger but not giving in.

"Stop," she said in a hoarse whisper.

The two girls stood still, their dresses pulled down to their waists and their shoes on the floor beside them.

Shada could feel Hollis's panic. He was still able to send signals to her body, but now the body wasn't responding. When he'd lost control before, he was banished to the darkness. Now, he lived in the light.

CHAPTER THIRTY-TWO

SHADA SPOKE AGAIN, this time with more force. "Stop. Put your clothes back on," she told the girls. While she controlled her mouth and vocal cords, Hollis was able to communicate with the rest of her body. She hadn't been back in control long enough to stop him.

Hollis threw her right hand onto the table and with the left gouged one of the wounds on her cheek. Three fingernails dug into her flesh, causing her eyes to roll back into her head.

The girls were terrified. Shada could sense their racing hearts and, using the resonation of her own heartbeat with theirs, was able to take back control of her hand and end the searing pain. She found her legs, forced herself to stand up, and walked into the bathroom.

"Don't go anywhere," Hollis snarled. He was able to take back control of Shada's voice while Shada was preoccupied controlling her movement.

Shada could feel Hollis try to retake control of her legs. The sensation was similar to a leg being asleep; she could still stand and move, but her body's response was slow.

When Hollis realized her legs were out of his reach, he took over her arms. She could tell when his attention switched to a different part of her body, but she wasn't fast enough to get there first. Hollis grabbed the backs of chairs, which fell over, and held onto the edge of the doorway in an attempt to stop Shada from reaching her destination. Shada's legs continued to march, and with some help from her momentum, she was able to continue despite Hollis's best attempts to stop her.

In the bathroom, Shada stared at her face in the mirror and focused on her pounding heart. At first, it felt like she was chasing Hollis from limb to limb, but once she accepted the impulses in totality, she gained a relaxed control over her entire body. Her fingers grazed the gashes on her cheeks. "Never again," she whispered. The marks had a new meaning now, that she was back in control of herself, constant reminders of the harm that could result from allowing someone else inside.

Shada felt Hollis try to blink and negated the signal. She heard a voice the world had lost during the upload: Hollis's. He muttered, "I can't even blink."

Shada smiled. "Didn't you tell me to smile more?" she thought.

"What are you talking about?" Shada heard. Her lips never moved.

She communicated via thoughts with the voice inside her head. "When we first met in the lab, you told me I should smile more. So here you go." Shada looked in the mirror and grinned, showing off as many teeth as she could. She allowed Hollis to see through her eyes without worrying if he could control where she looked.

Shada enjoyed Hollis's struggle. His attempts to find and control her limbs grew frantic, but none of the signals were anywhere near strong enough to overpower her. Her smile, forced at first, became genuine.

"What's the phrase to send the money to Sikya?" she thought.

Hollis refused to acknowledge her words and stayed silent. Shada knew she didn't need him to admit the phrase to her; she could read his thoughts. It wouldn't be hard to probe his memories.

She pried his mind open with little trouble. The process reminded her of trying to give her childhood dog his medicine, the insertion of a finger between teeth and a controlled effort to open his jaw wide enough to insert a pill. An initial struggle with no real threat of failure.

While Hollis's memory was under attack, he made no effort to control her body. It was as if his mind was frozen while under inspection.

The dancing dwarf.

"Thank you," Shada said to herself in the mirror. "I never would've guessed that."

Shada spent the next few minutes, an eternity for her, stopping Hollis from controlling any part of her body. She accepted his desires as she did other sensations, reducing him to a series of impulses. The process was similar to what all children undergo when learning to control their response to stimulation. Shada had learned to control her impulses once; it was easier to do as an adult.

Shada wasn't sure of the science behind what she was experiencing. She thought she'd understood after Alfie's explanation, but this new development didn't make sense. How could it be possible to experience both consciousnesses inside the same mind? The only explanation she could come up with was that Hollis's attempts at control were like flashes of light, or an entire mapping of lights, that she was able to extinguish at will. As long as she kept the flashes of light as short as possible, she could maintain control over her own body.

She wished she could tell Alfie so he could do further research and provide more clarity, but she would never reveal her secret. The injections would have to continue so Alfie didn't grow suspicious. Shada knew she could always find her own heartbeat's resonation with the world around her, aided by the low-dose LSD injections.

The injections didn't keep her mind in the darkness. They opened her awareness.

Shada, satisfied with her level of control, walked back out and told the girls, who hadn't moved in the half hour Shada had been gone, to put their clothes back on. She walked them back to the elevator and rode it to the surface with them.

Both girls stared at Shada's face during their vertical trip. It seemed like they were aware of the change in Shada, that this was another young girl in a strange place, just like them.

Shada felt a burst of energy and recognized another of Hollis's attempts to retake control. Shada couldn't tell if these attempts were becoming less powerful or if she had less of a reaction to them, but she was confident they wouldn't register in the near future. She dove into his memories. He tried to block her, but she was able to neutralize his resistance with brute force. She remembered, through Hollis's eyes, when he sat in Alfie's office and told the scientist the phrase he would have to say to release the funds. She wasn't sure how probing his memory served to freeze him, but she didn't care. All she cared about was that it worked.

One of the girls asked Shada what happened to her face.

"My shell cracked," Shada said. She flashed them a mischievous smile.

The girls seemed to understand what she meant and nodded in unison. All three hearts skipped a beat.

CHAPTER THIRTY-THREE

"I BET you're wondering how I got these scars," Shada said to the support group. Shada looked at the five members of the group and smiled at each one in turn. She wanted them to see she wasn't ashamed of the new additions to her face. The narrowing of her eyes tugged at the scabs on her face, causing pain on the upper part of her cheek.

She'd been in complete control of her body for a full two days. She'd asked Alfie to call the group together, telling the scientist it was so she could tell them what to expect if their host took over.

Shada did her best to place herself in Hollis's shoes before she spoke. "I did this to remind my host who's in charge." She flashed her best wicked grin.

The weasel-looking man, an edited mind placed into an edited body, leaned in. The others shifted in their seats. Not one of them offered words of support.

Shada thought the others didn't understand. Their silence pulled more words from her. "She tried to regain control and kill me!" she exclaimed.

The dark-haired man and woman, edited minds transplanted into unedited bodies, didn't look surprised at the news. The other two edited minds placed in edited bodies, the Asian woman and the man with the ponytail, shook their heads. "That isn't possible," the weasel said.

"Well, it happened to me!" Shada said, imagining herself to be Hollis telling the world about his struggle.

"To be clear, she's not suggesting you go to these lengths," Alfie clarified. "This response was uncalled for; we had already been able to suppress the host with an injection."

Shada nodded in agreement but thought Alfie was seeking acknowledgment for his serum. She wasn't going to give it to him. "Of course, there's no reason to go to this extreme. I just wanted to call out the elephant in the room." Everyone stared at Shada as if they didn't understand the metaphor.

"The reason I asked Alfie to bring everyone together again is because there are a few tricks I learned to maintain control, and I want you to be aware of them." She looked at the weasel, the Asian woman, and the man with the goatee. She doubted the edited minds trapped inside would be able to grasp the importance of what she was about to share but figured it wouldn't hurt them to listen, if they could. Her message was intended for the unedited whose bodies had been taken over by edited individuals, the same situation she herself faced with Hollis. She had to assume the unedited minds trapped inside had been able to see and hear the world of their bodies. So, while she looked at the three edited humans, she was really talking to the two dark-haired unedited people with deep-set eyes.

"Everyone close your eyes," she instructed. The group obeyed.

Alfie's questioning eyes stayed open, but he didn't object.

"First, we're going to imagine what it's like to have contact with your body taken away from you. Imagine you're at the bottom of a deep well. The circle of light in the distance, it's calling to you. Don't reach for it, allow it to take over your awareness. The process might be slow, but don't rush."

A few moments later, the broad-shouldered Asian woman opened her eyes. "I don't see anything. How's this supposed to help?"

"Trust me," Shada said.

She closed her eyes again and bowed her head.

"Then, once you've been able to find the light, allow the sounds of the world to rush in. It might take some time to find—"

"I'm still not seeing the light," the dark-haired man said.

"It's OK, this is just practice in case you find yourself losing control," Shada said, believing the unedited consciousness inside him knew what she was talking about. She closed her eyes and could sense the heartbeats of the two unedited humans, faint thrums she would miss if she wasn't looking for them. Even with her recent injection, it was difficult to maintain her awareness of them.

"Everyone open your eyes. So now, you're able to see and hear the world around you. I call this waking up." Shada didn't need to keep the group isolated from one another anymore. If the trapped minds heard her, they would be able to follow along in the background while the minds who had control were present in the room.

"But you'd still be trapped inside. The next thing to do would be to gain awareness of a background process without your host finding out. Take breathing, for example. Nobody gives it any thought, but thousands of times a day means a lot of opportunities for the trapped mind to find something to hold on to."

Alfie's eyes burrowed into Shada. She ignored the impulse to cater her explanation to him.

"With awareness comes control, and with control of a physical process, it isn't long before the rest of the body can be manipulated."

"We already have control of these bodies, we don't need to learn," the man with the goatee said.

"You're right, I just want you to be aware of the threat posed. But if your host ever tries to take back control of their bodies, you can use these strategies to maintain the status quo."

The heartbeats of the dark-haired man and woman grew louder. Now Shada couldn't miss them if she tried.

Shada did her best to sound as commanding as Hollis. "If it does happen, make sure you get into Alfie's lab as soon as possible so he can use the serum he developed to put them back in place."

The three edited humans looked confused. Shada guessed the edited minds inside their bodies would never pose a risk of taking over. But the other two, their hearts began to race.

Shada assumed they had found their breath and were overjoyed at the prospect of removing the chains of the edited mind. She allowed her heartbeat to resonate with theirs, slowing them down. "All this is to say: don't take drastic action against your body, like putting two gashes into your face," she said with a smile.

"Don't cause massive self-harm, got it," the weasel said. "Can we go? I've got a lot of work to do."

Alfie looked at Shada, telling her to field the question without saying so. "We're almost done. Last question: Is anyone suspicious their host is trying to take back control?"

The two unedited humans raised their hands. The woman's hand shot back down, and she stared at it hanging useless by her side. The man stared at his raised hand, and it was clear he was exerting a large effort to keep it aloft.

"At least two hosts here are trying to take back control. Alfie, get the serum."

The three edited humans gawked at the two members of the group who were struggling to keep control of their hands. Shada couldn't sense their heartbeats and determined they would forever be silent. Edited minds in edited bodies posed no risk to be lost.

Alfie injected both unedited humans with the serum, and a wave of relaxation washed over each of their faces. "I've had a sense of foreboding for some time now," the man said.

"And when they found out there was a serum to keep them in the darkness, they had to show themselves," Shada said. She took a weird pride in having the edited minds present believe she was on their side. While she smiled in their faces, she was also resonating her heartbeat with the two unedited, showing them the true path to subversion. Soon they would be able to follow their blood, the path to accepting the implanted mind as another part of themselves, giving them the ability to take back their bodies without struggling to keep a separate mind silent.

The entire group watched the two unedited humans, in possession of edited minds, to see if there were any signs of struggle. They looked at the group around them and smiled.

"Nothing?" Alfie asked.

"Nothing," they said, shaking their heads.

Shada alone knew the unedited minds trapped inside were now learning to listen to their own heartbeats, and it was just a matter of time before they hatched.

CHAPTER THIRTY-FOUR

THE TIME HAD COME for Shada to make sure Sikya received the promised funds, but doing so meant she would have to do her best impression of Hollis. It had been some time since Hollis had tried to take control of any part of her body, but she knew he was aware of her actions, a constant presence on the periphery of her awareness.

Shada took a big breath outside Alfie's office to calm her nerves. She walked into the scientist's office and sat down. "First things first. Let's get the money sent over to the host's sister," she said.

Alfie leaned back in his chair and steepled his fingers. "Are you sure you want to do that?"

"The dancing dwarf," Shada said. She made sure it was said both with confidence and in an offhanded way, a simple matter of business they needed to address.

Alfie smiled before he leaned forward and typed on his computer. "We should go for a walk," he said when he finished. He led the way back to and through the atrium then outside, towards the lab. He didn't call a transport vehicle. "Nobody can hear us out here."

"Who is listening inside?"

"I don't want any record of this conversation, even on my own devices," Alfie said. He turned to Shada and stared into her eyes. "Welcome back," he said with a smile.

Shada pretended she was Hollis. "I've been back since the injection!"

Alfie nodded and continued to walk along the outside of the building. Shada followed.

"I told the people at accounting to release the funds to your sister, so you don't have to worry about that hanging over your head. Would you like to call her and confirm?" he said.

"Why would I want to talk to an unedited?" Shada tried to sound disgusted at the thought, although to the best of her recollection Hollis didn't speak about them in this way. He'd known she was unedited when they first met and was nice enough to her. Still, the tone seemed right.

"Hollis didn't have a negative view of the unedited. In his eyes, he thought he would be helping them by offering them the ability to become edited. It was pity, not disgust."

Shada didn't know what to say. How would someone respond if they were told their own views on a topic? Alfie spoke again before Shada could probe Hollis's thoughts.

"Shada, I know it's you." His eyes stayed forward. "I thought you'd be the one to do it."

Shada refused to admit she had taken back control of her own body, scared Alfie would come up with another serum. The palm trees swayed in the breeze brought in by the bay. An automated lawn mower in front of a warehouse in the distance turned on a dime and began another straight line over the grass.

"The serum was my best attempt at keeping you subdued. Correct me if I'm wrong, but now that you've been able to overpower Hollis despite the injections, there's really no chance he's coming back. What's the secret? How'd you do it?"

They took a dozen more steps towards the bay in the distance before Shada responded. "I learned to listen."

Alfie waited, but Shada didn't continue. "Very well, don't go into specifics. Just know that I won't do anything more to stop you. If you were able to pry the phrase from Hollis's mind, there are levels to this I don't understand. Maybe one day you'll trust me enough to share."

"Why would I trust you?" Shada said. She felt comfortable saying this because she still didn't have to admit it was her, not Hollis.

"You shouldn't. But this has been my greatest experiment. I tried five times before you and none of them showed any promise. It wouldn't surprise me if one of them tried to retake control after your tutorial."

"The serum will put them back," Shada said.

"It will, but my hope is that you told them enough to overpower that too. My real experiment, the one WestCorp doesn't know about, was to see if a mind could be consumed by another human. Not under their control—we do that every time someone uploads for a few hours at a time—but in a way that allows their entire database of knowledge and experiences to be retrieved at will. By telling me the phrase, you proved it was possible, although to what extent I don't yet know."

Shada felt Hollis try to take control of her voice, to scream at Alfie, then her hands, to attack him. Fueled by rage, these impulses were more powerful than his previous attempts, but they were still received by Shada as nuisances to be ignored. She had stopped walking for a moment, and Alfie looked back at her from a few steps ahead.

"Like watching a storm pass," he said in admiration.

Shada nodded, took the few steps to close the distance between them, and they continued to walk.

"Do you get constant input from two sources of knowledge?

Or is it more like you have to retrieve Hollis's knowledge, like a massive encyclopedia you must search every time you have a question?"

"Two inputs would be overwhelming," Shada said, still wary.

"So you have to know the question you want answered before you dive into his mind. Fascinating."

Alfie pointed to the building behind the lawn mower. "What's that building used for?"

Shada dove into Hollis's memories and knew the answer in less than the time it took to blink. "It's where edited children go to primary school." If Hollis was still in control of her body, he would know the answer, so she had no reservations about answering the question.

Alfie pointed to a smaller building near the water. "And that one?"

"The administration offices for the marketing department."

"They're the ones who advertise to the unedited. The reason you came, if I'm not mistaken."

Shada nodded. "Will you upload an edited mind into an unedited body again?"

"Of course! What kind of scientist would I be if I didn't produce repeatable results?"

Shada shook her head, unwilling to speak up for the future victims of the procedure.

"There's another option as well. One that I believe you are uniquely suited for," Alfie said.

"And what is that?"

"We upload another mind into your body. You've regained control once, doing it again should prove no more difficult."

Shada was unable to control her first impulse. "Why the hell would I let you do that?"

"Think about it. Multiple minds, multiple databases, all

searchable in an instant. You already have all the resources you could ever want, but their resources would be yours as well. You could have multiple lives' worth of knowledge at your fingertips. A true superhuman."

Shada stopped walking and stared at Alfie. "I'm going back," she said. She turned around and left the scientist alone in the realm of possibility.

CHAPTER THIRTY-FIVE

SHADA COULDN'T SHAKE Alfie's suggestion to probe Hollis's memory when viewing the world around her. As she entered the atrium, she half remembered its initial construction. It had been sterile and empty when the foreman led Hollis into the space and announced the project's completion. The tram station underneath, a direct line to the city, had been completed soon after. Before that, there had been a ferry that brought employees to the island. They were more isolated then and liked it that way, a small group of visionaries trying to change the world with technology. Hollis had ignored their grievances when he connected them to the outside world.

On the way to Hollis's underground bunker, she remembered a time before the automated vehicles ran between buildings. They used to have to walk! Hollis's memory included a time being caught in a rainstorm, and a massive swell flooding the underground cavern before it was complete.

Shada was aware of Hollis's memories everywhere she went, small tidbits of information about the world around her. If she wasn't careful to ground herself in reality, to pay attention to her surroundings, it was easy to get caught in a sense of nostalgia about a world long since passed. She cursed Alfie for opening up Pandora's box.

The underground bunker took on a new significance once Shada became aware of Hollis's reason for creating the space. Numerous death threats had been made against him for his work editing unborn children. A fanatic from the city had come to the island and hid until the middle of the night, well after the tram stopped running. Hollis woke up to find the man holding a knife to his throat while Ruby slept next to him; his children, a boy and a girl, were in rooms down the hall. He'd had the bunker created and moved in alone in order to protect his family.

Feeling sorry for Hollis felt wrong, but Shada couldn't help it. His own story, now present as she moved through the residence, made her appreciate all he had done. When faced with a similar situation, she might have done the same.

The black wall behind the long table between the kitchen and the bedroom drew Shada's gaze. She remembered the hours Hollis had spent in front of that wall. It wasn't just his actions Shada remembered, but also his thoughts, and she became aware of how Hollis had found the black wall comforting while he pondered his status as edited, wondering if there were aspects of life he was missing out on because of his inability to feel sadness. It reminded Shada of a child's curiosity when looking at the stars, the light bouncing off the textured rock filling him with wonder at the unknown.

Shada called Hollis's office.

Beth answered the phone after the first ring, prompting Shada to wonder if she knew the call was from his living quarters. If the secretary was surprised to hear Shada's voice, she hid it well.

"Can you please send Chloe Rose down to Hollis's bunker? She's unedited but is staying on the island for testing," Shada said. Shada wondered if she would ever be comfortable claiming Hollis's belongings as her own, though she knew she had to continue to pretend they belonged to him as long as people didn't know his mind resided in her.

"Chloe Rose, got it," Beth replied, sounding as if she was writing down the name.

"Tell her I'll be waiting behind the outdoor structure, next to the water."

Beth said she would relay the message right away.

Shada went back outside and walked to the water's edge. There was no sand. Instead, the ground dropped away a few feet where water had eroded the island, exposing soil that extended into the water. The water was too dark to see anything beneath. The wind picked up speed, keeping Shada cool beneath the setting sun. She dove into Hollis's memories and discovered a time when he had been a young edited member of the island community. He'd wanted to explore the depths of the ocean even though he was assigned to explore the depths of the mind. Shada felt pity for young Hollis, born into a society that took away his right to determine his own future.

"Hello?" Chloe called from behind her.

Shada turned around and was greeted by an apprehensive Chloe. She no longer had the jewelry in her pierced septum, but her earlobes, exposed by the wind blowing back her hair, still showed numerous pieces of metal.

Shada closed the distance between them with a few long strides. "You're not hijacked right now, are you?" she asked.

"No . . ." Chloe said.

"Then who am I?"

"You're Hollis, inside Shada's body."

"So you remember my name. That's good," Shada said with a laugh.

Chloe didn't even smile.

"It's me! Shada!" She threw her hands out as if to put herself on display.

Chloe's head turned sideways. "You're Shada?" She got defensive. "What is this, some kind of trick? Your body was taken over by Hollis."

"It was. But he's in the background now. I taught myself to take back control of my body."

"I don't believe you. What did we do the first night you came over?"

"We followed the police scanner to the warehouses."

Chloe thought for a moment. "They could have been following you." She still wasn't convinced.

"That's true." Shada thought for a moment. "What about the poison you inject yourself with before each upload? If Hollis knew about that, there's no way he would allow you to host his wife's mind."

Chloe's eyes grew wide. "Holy shit, it is you!" She rushed forward and gave her friend a hug. "What the hell happened to your face?"

"Hollis wasn't happy I took back control of my body. He left these before I was able to make my control permanent."

Chloe leaned in close to inspect the two thin lines. "Well, they look cool," she said with a smile.

Shada dismissed the compliment with a wave of her hand. "Let's go inside. I want to show you how this guy lived."

From the moment they got off the elevator, Chloe rushed from room to room. "This was all his? It's all yours?" Chloe asked as she stood in front of Shada in the kitchen after her inspection of the residence. "How does that work? Do you call everything yours now, or do you still think of it as his?"

"I still think of it as his," Shada said. She leaned her lower back on the counter. "And it was all his. This was his home."

Chloe looked up at the roof of the cavern in awe. "How'd you do it?"

"Take back my body?"

Chloe nodded.

"Have you been able to see or hear the world while being hijacked?" Shada asked.

"Not until the most recent one. I saw you, and heard your voice, but was so sad knowing you were occupied by another mind and would never be the person I remembered. I had to convince myself you were dead."

"Good, that's the first step."

"Pretending who you see is dead?"

"No, seeing and hearing the world while you're hijacked."

Chloe pulled a chair from beneath the table and sat down. "And what do you do after that?"

"Well, I started by finding my breath and controlling it. It leads to one level of control by shutting off the hijacker's mind. It's hard to maintain though and requires constant focus on breathing."

Chloe held her breath even though she wasn't hosting another mind. She exhaled and displayed a sheepish grin. "So are you focusing on your breath right now?"

"No need, I don't have to keep Hollis muted." Shada was struck by the thought that Hollis's residence could have listening devices but an instant later was calmed by the knowledge, from the owner himself, that Hollis valued privacy too much to allow their installation. "He's with me all the time."

"How'd you do that?"

"Listened to my heartbeat. It led to an awareness of every part of my body. Now, even when Hollis does try to take over, I can brush his attempts away."

Chloe became silent, and Shada could tell she was trying to detect her own heart.

"That seems hard," Chloe said.

"The injections helped," Shada said. She went on to explain how the low dose of LSD had helped her become aware of the life in everything around her, a sensation that tore away her ability to focus on her breathing but opened a new avenue for her to explore.

"So what are you going to do now? Live down here and become a recluse?"

"No way, I'm leaving. We just came down here because I wanted you to see the way this guy lives and to get my stuff."

Shada went into the bedroom and grabbed her bag. She changed out of the WestCorp clothes and put back on her shorts, sports bra, and T-shirt. They all smelled like stale sweat. At the bottom of her backpack was the apple she'd taken from her apartment, still red and shiny. Thoughts of Sikya bubbled up in Shada's mind and she felt a wave of homesickness in her stomach. Shada shouldered the backpack and walked back into the kitchen.

"Are you going back to the city?" Chloe asked.

Shada nodded. "I need to see Sikya. Are you going back to the dorms?"

"Only to get my things. I'm coming with you."

CHAPTER THIRTY-SIX

CHLOE AND SHADA left the bunker and were greeted by the last remnants of the day. The waves lapping against the shore underlined the purple, orange, and red hues created by single rays of sunshine. They took the transport vehicle Chloe had used to get to the bunker back to the atrium.

"I'll have to come back. I still need the money," Chloe said during the ride.

"I've got all the money you'll ever need," Shada said. "All of Hollis's accounts were signed over to me."

"That's a nice offer, but I can't accept. It's your money. Use it for yourself, and Sikya."

"Sikya got money too. We have more than we need. Let me help you," Shada said. "Plus, you've already been hijacked more times than anyone else. It's not safe to do it again."

"I'll be fine," Chloe said. She sighed. "And it's not just the money. Part of me wants to know if I can do what you did. I know it's not a competition, but I think I can control a mind that's been transplanted into my body. What if we take over multiple people? We could each have access to not only their funds, but lifetimes of knowledge. Imagine what we could do!"

Shada turned to stare at Chloe. "There's no guarantee it can be done again. What if I just got lucky?"

"Well, let me be the one to find out. If your method works, we don't have to be the only ones. Imagine all the edited minds we could capture! It would be a double blow. Unedited minds becoming more powerful while taking out the edited humans at the top. We could flip the world."

Shada knew Chloe's logic was sound but didn't want her friend to risk being lost to the world forever. She stared out the window and could sense Hollis's anger at his helplessness. They arrived at the atrium while she listened to the captured consciousness inside her.

"Go get your stuff and meet me above the steps at the entrance to the station," Shada told Chloe from outside the transport.

Chloe nodded, told Shada she'd be right back, and the vehicle pulled away.

Shada walked inside. In the seating area, with a tray full of food in front of her, was Piper. The edited woman stood up and walked towards Shada, leaving her food behind. A furrowed brow was perched on her contorted face, and each step was further evidence of her iron resolve.

Piper stopped in front of Shada. The two of them stood at the entrance to the island's coffee shop. "Where has he been?" she demanded to know. When Shada didn't respond right away, she placed both hands on her hips and stared as if her eyes had the power to force someone to talk. "Well?" she said.

"What makes you think I'd know?" Shada said. Her calm exterior hid how ready she was for Piper to strike.

"I spoke with Beth and Ernie, all they'll tell me is he isn't in the office. You and Alfie are the only two allowed into his residence, and Alfie won't see me."

At the mention of Alfie's name Shada was struck by one of

Hollis's memories. Alfie, it turned out, was Hollis's son. The scientist had changed his name when he received his doctorate, a practice Shada learned was common among the scientists.

Lost in a fog of the past, Shada tried to walk away from Piper and leave the conversation behind. Piper grabbed her arm to stop her. Shada was pulled back to the present. She stared at the hand and knew it would be easy to overpower the woman.

Piper let go.

"He's been sick in bed, if you must know. The only reason I go down there is so he can upload. It gives him the chance to move around."

"That's it? He's not having you do anything else?"

"What else could I do? I'm still not edited," Shada said. She knew Piper was worried about being replaced as lieutenant.

It took a second before Piper appeared to believe Shada. Her face relaxed and she let out a sigh. "I feel like he's up to something. I haven't heard from him for over a week now . . ." Her voice trailed off.

Shada could tell Piper wasn't satisfied with the response she got, that she wanted more information and was trying to gain Shada's trust to find out what she wanted to know.

"Nothing I'd know about," Shada said.

Piper's eyes narrowed in renewed suspicion, but there was nothing else she could do. She walked away without another word.

Shada took a seat near the steps that led down to the tram station and set her backpack on a chair next to her. She watched the edited humans visit the various restaurants, wondering if they ate every meal in the food court or if any of them cooked their own food. Hollis didn't seem to know the answer; when Shada probed his consciousness, she found out the leader of WestCorp had been brought all his meals precooked. He didn't know or care about the rest of the island's occupants.

An older woman, near seventy, caught Shada's eye. She carried a tray with a covered plate on it and was given a wide berth by all the edited humans in her vicinity. Hollis remembered the woman and Shada discovered her identity: Ruby, Hollis's wife.

Shada was flooded with memories of their time together. She already knew they'd lived in a spacious house on the island next to the water, where they raised their two children. After Hollis moved to the underground bunker, the two of them had drifted apart and never lived together again. Hollis harbored no ill will toward the woman; they'd just fallen out of their routine and never got back into one that involved the other.

Chloe came from behind Shada and sat at the table with her. "You just missed Piper," Shada said.

Chloe pretended to be upset. "No! I really wanted to catch up." She laughed. "What did she want?"

"Hollis was planning to upload into her before I came along. She thinks I have some grand plan to take over the company and wanted to double-check I wasn't becoming his number two. She's got a weird protective thing about him."

Shada could sense Hollis wanted to look at Ruby again, and she obliged. "Do you see the old woman over there?" Shada asked, gesturing with her chin towards Ruby.

"The one sitting by herself?" Chloe said, turning away from Shada to look at the topic of their conversation.

"That's Ruby Hollis," Shada said.

Chloe stared at the woman who had taken over her mind. "She's a slow eater," Chloe said.

Shada watched Ruby take two bites. Each one took minutes.

Ruby must have sensed their eyes, because she lifted her own, looked in their direction, and stared at the two of them. The fork with her next bite hovered in front of her face. Chloe turned back around, but Shada didn't avert her gaze.

Ruby never took the bite. She set the fork down and beckoned for someone sitting at the next table to come to her. The man who came to her side had a mustache. When he leaned over, Ruby whispered something into his ear. The man turned and looked at Shada and Chloe.

"Shit," Shada said.

"What's wrong?" Chloe asked.

"We have to go." Shada stood up and slung her backpack over her shoulder.

Chloe followed Shada's lead.

"What's wrong?" Chloe repeated.

"You said you were able to witness the visit in Hollis's office, right?"

"It was the first time I wasn't in complete darkness."

"So you know Ruby knows that Hollis transplanted his mind into my body." As Shada said this, she led the way to the stairs and took them two at a time. The last thing she saw in the atrium was the man with a mustache beckoning for the men from the surrounding tables to come to him.

"There's no reason for Hollis to be in the atrium," Chloe said.

"And even less of a reason for him to be seated with an unedited, unless I've been able to take back control. She knows."

CHAPTER THIRTY-SEVEN

SHADA AND CHLOE weaved through commuters waiting to go to the city for the night. Although there were more people on the platform than Shada had seen before—their exodus coincided with the end of the business day on the island—there was enough room to pass through the crowd without jostling anyone. They were careful not to maintain a brisk walk so they wouldn't garner suspicion as they put as much distance between themselves and the staircase as possible.

Shada kept looking behind her to see if they were being pursued. Each time she looked at the staircase, all she saw were the two security guards, one on each side of the bottom step. She worried they would receive orders to stop her and Chloe, but from their unaffected stare, she could tell the two of them would be staying put.

On the far end of the platform, they stopped to wait for the tram to arrive. A few tense minutes later, a low grumble came from the tunnel that extended towards the center of the island, soon followed by a pair of lights. A rush of air in front of the tram blew through the crowd until the tram's first car stopped in front of Shada and Chloe. Chloe brushed the hair from her face, and Shada clutched the straps of her backpack while her eyes still watched the staircase.

The doors opened and they boarded. As the doors shut behind them, Shada allowed herself to exhale. The tram began to move. Shada took one last look at the staircase and saw the mustached man reach the platform. He seemed to be in no rush whatsoever. The two security guards lifted their massive frames from their seats when they recognized the man who'd missed the trip into the city. Shada saw the mustached man lift a finger in their direction before she left the station and the tunnel's wall blocked her view.

The tram then came to an abrupt stop. Everyone on board was thrust forward when their momentum was interrupted. One man, whose hands weren't fast enough to catch himself, smashed his face into the seat in front of his own. He yelped in pain and sat back up with blood dripping through the hands covering his face.

Shada probed Hollis's mind. "They are able to stop and reverse the tram," she whispered to Chloe.

Chloe searched the area around her, and Shada presumed she was looking for a weapon. Not finding anything to use for defense, Chloe took out a vial of the poison and offered it to Shada.

"Just in case," Chloe said.

Shada shook her head no.

The tram began to continue on towards the city. It inched along as if it was unsure of its trajectory. It soon picked up speed, and moments later the passengers found themselves passing above the bay in the reflected light of the moon.

Shada's first guess was that Alfie had had something to do with the tram not going back to the island, but the scientist would have no way of knowing she had left. After further consideration, she came up with the theory that after the mustached man had stopped the tram, Ruby had overruled the reversal and allowed her to escape. She felt her instincts were correct but had no idea why Ruby would interject on her behalf.

Shada leaned back in her seat but was unable to relax. She refused to believe she had been able to escape the island until the city was close enough for her to distinguish individual buildings in the night, and even then she wasn't convinced. When the tram descended into the tunnel below the city she became nervous, knowing her destination was close. She believed that once she got into the city, her nightmare would be over and she could disappear into the mass of unedited.

She could tell Hollis, his mind trapped in her body, was excited about the prospect of living among the unedited. He relished the opportunity to see firsthand how they lived. Shada knew he held out hope that he would one day regain control of her body, and his time among the people would allow him to further understand those he wished to eliminate as part of his company's grand vision.

Chloe seemed to share Shada's reservations. It was obvious she was on edge as well, waiting to see if they would be allowed to reach the city.

The tram pulled to a stop below the hub of the city. Shada and Chloe stood by the door, and as soon as it opened they fell onto the platform, the first passengers to disembark. Free from the long reach of WestCorp, they gave each other a hug. They didn't care that the rest of the passengers stared at them.

Shada and Chloe went up a level to the city's transportation system. Shada assumed the two of them would be parting ways, but Chloe announced she was going with Shada.

"I want to make sure you get home," she said with finality, as if this phrase was enough explanation to put the matter to rest.

Shada didn't put up a fight. Chloe allowed Shada to have the last open seat on the train and stood over her as they rode to

Shada's stop. They got off, and Shada saw the homeless man with his dog. Remembering the apple in her backpack, she took it out. Its skin was still shiny, red, and tight. Instead of giving it away, which she didn't want to do because she knew the homeless man would just set it off to the side, she took a bite.

The apple was rotten on the inside, dark brown and mushy. Now that its skin had been pierced, a putrid smell wafted out, covering the area around her. She spit it out onto the concrete below her.

"What the hell," Shada said. She spit, trying to get the taste from her mouth, but it didn't help.

Chloe looked at the apple in Shada's hand. "Why'd you eat a rotten apple?" she said.

"It didn't look rotten!" Shada said in defense. She turned the apple to show Chloe the fruit from the unbitten side. Its color was still bright red, but now that its skin had been pierced, the rest of the skin was wrinkled, like a drum that had been cut.

"How old was it?"

Shada threw the apple over the fence and onto the track below, which ran perpendicular to the station. "A few weeks, I guess. It's the one I took from the apartment."

"And you expected it to still be good?"

"It looked good on the outside." Shada spit on the ground again. "This is why I stick to gummy bears."

CHAPTER THIRTY-EIGHT

SHADA KNEW Sikya was home as she and Chloe approached the apartment door. She didn't have a specific reason why she knew—there was no audible activity behind the locked door— and couldn't elaborate her reasons if she had to, but deep down she knew her sister was there. Call it a sister's intuition. She didn't consider what Sikya thought about her last disappearance until she was about to knock. She wondered if her sister would be upset when they saw each other again after she'd left just a one-word note as her final goodbye and had had no contact since leaving. She got the urge to turn around and walk away, to save the reunion for another time, but didn't move.

Chloe, perhaps sensing Shada's reservation, told her friend, "Sikya's going to be happy you're back."

"I don't know. She probably wasn't happy I left."

"Trust me," Chloe said.

Shada knocked twice, even though she had a key.

A shadow passed beneath the door. All of a sudden, the locks were disengaged and the door flew open. A breathless Sikya stood in the doorway, concern written on her face.

"What happened to your face?" Sikya asked.

While Shada stumbled to find the right words, Sikya rushed out and wrapped her sister in her arms. Sikya squeezed tightly and pushed her chin into Shada's neck, a pressure that disarmed Shada and assuaged any concerns she'd had about any imagined animosity her sister might have felt. The two held each other a long time before they parted and Sikya held her sister at arm's length.

"Are those lines supposed to be some sort of tattoo?" Sikya asked.

Shada shook her head and laughed at her sister's naivety. "It's a long story."

Inside Shada, Hollis felt a sadistic pride at leaving his mark on what he considered his property. Shada didn't bother to correct him about who her body belonged to.

Sikya introduced herself to Chloe and told the two of them to come inside.

"I can't stay for long, I just wanted to make sure she got back all right," Chloe said.

"Well, thanks for bringing her back!" Sikya said, turning it into a joke.

Shada tossed her backpack on the floor next to the couch and sat down, the weight of her time away hitting her and pressing down, making even the weight of gravity intolerable. Chloe chose to stand with her lower back against the counter.

Sikya sat down next to her sister. "Where were you?" she asked.

"On the island."

Sikya let the information sink in. "I thought you went overseas."

"My playing career is over," Shada said. She hadn't really thought about it before that moment, but without the need for money, there was no incentive to fight for the chance to play in the league. Her love for the sport was still there, but she didn't want to fight against an unfair system.

Reminded of money, Shada told Sikya to check her account.

"It says there's a pending transfer," Sikya said, trailing off. A moment later she gasped and set down her phone. "Shada. What did you do to get that much money?"

Shada ignored her sister's question. "That's just the money for you. I have my own, much more than that."

Shada explained how Sikya's money had come from Hollis's payment for uploading himself into her body. When Sikya said she knew this, Shada had to tell her it was meant to be permanent. That it was permanent. "His mind is in my body right now," Shada said.

Sikya's eyes grew wide. "You said sorry because you weren't coming back." She grew agitated. "What were you thinking!"

Shada watched her sister stand up and pace in front of the couch. "It's not important. I'm back now," she said.

Chloe had heard enough. She cleared her throat and announced she was leaving, going back home.

Shada stood up. "Promise me you won't go back."

Chloe smiled. "I promise."

The two friends hugged each other and Chloe left. As soon as the door shut behind her, Sikya announced Chloe was lying. "You could see it in her eyes."

Shada was surprised Sikya was able to tell, since they'd just met each other for the first time. "Agreed. She thinks she can capture another edited mind. Then we'd both have access to a lifetime of knowledge and resources."

"You know everything the guy inside your head knows?"

Shada nodded with a sly smile on her face.

"Is that why you did it?" Sikya said. "Like a robbery?"

"No, I had no idea I could take over again. I thought I would be effectively dead."

"And you still followed through with the procedure! What's wrong with you?"

"I left you a note!" Shada said. It was meant to be a joke, but Sikya didn't find it funny.

Shada struggled with whether or not to tell her sister her ability to get a birth license was on the line. "I did it so you never have to worry about money again. But having been on that island all this time, and seeing what WestCorp plans to do, you have to promise not to edit any child you have."

Sikya grew suspicious. "What does WestCorp plan to do?"

"They are going to force all births to be edited. The mayor and everything's involved."

Sikya sat back down on the couch, the new information and her own weight too much to bear. "What's going to happen when people refuse?"

"They will be offered cheap post-birth edits so they won't feel the pain of being childless."

Sikya let this revelation soak in before she spoke again. "So I won't be able to have an unedited child," she uttered, her sadness filling up the room.

"As of right now, no. Not officially at least. But we have all the money we could ever want, so there has to be someone we can pay."

Sikya shook her head. "I don't want it if others don't have the same opportunity." She set her jaw, and her eyes narrowed with determination. "We have some work to do," she said.

Sikya had every reason to turn her back on the people of her city, but she chose to fight for them, even though her sister would have preferred to leave them to their fate. Without people like Sikya, people who fought against the natural order, the world would never evolve.

With technology creating such a clear line between those with and without edits, the ability to get inside the minds of those on the other side was a distinct advantage. Capturing the mind altogether, as Shada had, could, Sikya hoped, serve the same purpose.

The laws of evolution didn't account for adaptations being passed on instead of passed down.

ABOUT THE AUTHOR

Marcos Antonio Hernandez writes from the suburbs of Washington, D.C. An avid reader of both fiction and non-fiction, his favorite authors are Haruki Murakami and Philip K. Dick -- in that order.

Marcos graduated from the University of Maryland, College Park with a degree in chemical engineering and a minor in physics. Since graduating, he has worked as a barista, a food scientist, and a CrossFit coach.

Awakening is Marcos's fourth novel.

authormarcoshernandez.com

Made in the USA
Middletown, DE
02 June 2021